JUST IN TIME

Stories to Mark the Millennium

PUFFIN BOOKS

PUFFIN BOOKS

Published by the Penguin Group
Penguin Books Ltd, 27 Wrights Lane, London w8 5tz, England
Penguin Putnam Inc., 375 Hudson Street, New York, New York 10014, USA
Penguin Books Australia Ltd, Ringwood, Victoria, Australia
Penguin Books Canada Ltd, 10 Alcorn Avenue, Toronto, Ontario, Canada m4v 3b2
Penguin Books (NZ) Ltd, Private Bag 102902, NSMC, Auckland, New Zealand

Penguin Books Ltd, Registered Offices: Harmondsworth, Middlesex, England

First published 1999

3 5 7 9 10 8 6 4 2

Set in 14/18pt Monotype Bembo
Typeset by Rowland Phototypesetting Ltd,
Bury St Edmunds, Suffolk
Printed in England by Clays Ltd, St Ives plc

British Library Cataloguing in Publication Data
A CIP catalogue record for this book is available from the British Library

ISBN 0-141-30418-9

CONTENTS

Dick King-Smith

JULIUS CAESAR'S GOAT

Ancient Rome, 49–36 BC

*At school, I spent many years 'learning Latin'.
As a farmer I kept a number of goats. Somehow,
somewhen, these two facts came together in my
brain, and thinking about the exploits of the great
general and the rank smell of the male of the genus
Capra produced 'Julius Caesar's Goat'.*

You might think you knew quite a bit about
Julius Caesar. I bet you didn't know that
he had absolutely no sense of smell.

Though his parents were not all that bright –
his father's name was Crassus Idioticus and his
mother was called Stupida – Julius was in fact
a quick-witted boy, with excellent hearing and
twenty-twenty vision, but from the age of ten

onwards he couldn't smell a thing. He couldn't smell bread baking or meat roasting, and the scent of flowers meant nothing to him.

It happened like this.

Julius, who had been born in the year 100 BC, was playing with a lot of other boys in the playground at North Rome Primary School. It was 15 March (the Ides of March, the Romans called it) 90 BC and they were playing with a large, round ball made of a cow's stomach packed with scraps of rags from old togas.

The game was called Foot-the-Ball, and the idea was to kick it between two posts. The only person allowed to touch the ball with his hands was called the Keeper of the Goal, and that is what Caesar was that particular morning.

There was a great flurry in the mouth of the goal and one of Julius's opponents, a rough boy called Brutus, took a spectacular overhead kick at the ball and missed it. His foot hit Julius smack on the nose.

'*Et tu, Brute!*' cried Julius (which, loosely translated, means 'It would be you, you brute!') and he retired, hurt.

Stupida was horrified when her son arrived home, his handsome Roman nose all swollen – so swollen, in fact, that even Crassus Idioticus noticed.

But the swelling went down and Julius's nose looked much as it had before, apart from a slight bend in the middle. But it didn't work. Julius Caesar had lost his sense of smell, for ever.

They took him to all the best medical men in Rome, sparing no expense, but none could help, though one, the oldest and wisest, said to Julius, 'You must count your blessings, young man. The world may be full of pleasant smells, but it is also filled with horrible stinks and stenches, which now will never worry you.'

Julius Caesar never forgot this wise old man's remark, and many years later, when he was already a famous soldier, he used his handicap to great advantage.

In 49 BC he was commanding an army in Gaul and decided to attack another army led by a man called Pompey. To do this, he had to cross a stream called the Rubicon.

On the banks of this stream was a herd of

goats, which Caesar's legionaries, always eager for fresh meat, quickly killed and butchered. Amongst the nanny goats was one very large billy goat with long ginger hair and a pair of fine sweeping horns which broke free from the slaughterers and ran, bleating loudly, towards Julius Caesar himself as he strode down to the water's edge, surrounded by his bodyguard.

Hastily the bodyguard drew back because of the appalling smell that the billy goat gave out. All billy goats stink, but this one was a champion stinker.

Then a brave centurion stepped forward. 'O Caesar!' he cried. 'Wilt thou have this beast for lunch?' and he waited, sword upraised, his eyes on his leader's right hand.

If Caesar's thumb had then been turned down, one swipe would have removed the animal's head from its body.

Caesar looked down at the billy goat. He was impressed by the look in its eyes, a look much more intelligent than that of Crassus Idioticus or Stupida.

Meanwhile, the watching soldiers marvelled.

There was Caesar, standing right by the stinking creature, even laying his hand upon its head!

'O great Caesar!' they whispered to each other. 'What courage!'

Little did they know that he couldn't smell a thing.

Still the brave centurion waited, his sword upraised, holding his nose with the other hand.

Then Caesar said, '*Hircus audens est*' (which, loosely translated, means, 'That goat's got bottle'), and he put his thumb up.

The centurion lowered his sword, and Julius Caesar, closely followed by his goat, waded into the water and crossed the Rubicon.

Now, as his legions prepared to march south to confront the army of Pompey, Caesar issued an edict with regard to his new pet. Caesar's goat was to be accorded all possible honour, and anyone found guilty of treating it with disrespect would be put to death. As for the man who would have executed the animal if the general's thumb had turned down, he, much to his dismay, was appointed Centurion-Capricorn. Not even a rise in pay of one *denarius per diem* could compensate him for having now to live permanently in close proximity to that awful pong, but of course he could not complain.

'*Caesus durus!*' his mates whispered to him (which, loosely translated, means, 'Hard cheese!').

Now, as the legions moved south, Julius Caesar and his bodyguard, along with the Centurion-Capricorn and the animal itself, marched in the middle of the column of soldiers. The wind was in the north and thus blew upon their backs. It was a strong wind, so all those marching behind Caesar were in luck, for they were spared the smell of the billy goat. All those ahead of Caesar, however, caught the full impact of the wind-borne stink.

But then someone among these forward troops had a brilliant idea.

'If only that goat marched in front of us,' he said, 'right at the head of the column, the wind would carry the smell away from us too.'

Then someone else had an even more brilliant idea.

'What if Pompey's army were ahead of us? If

we were free of the stink and they were being suffocated by it? Why, before they'd recovered from the shock, we could make mincemeat of them!'

'By Jupiter! They'd all be gasping and choking, like we are now, and their eyes would be running, like ours are now, and they wouldn't be able to fight for toffee!'

'Yes, but how can we persuade Caesar to put the brute at the head of the army? "Why?" he'd say, and we couldn't say, "Because it stinks so bad." That'd be disrespect and we'd be topped.'

'What can we do then?'

'I know!' said a smarmy little legionary called Oleaginus. 'Leave it to me. I'll fix it.'

That night when they set up camp, Oleaginus made his way to Julius Caesar's tent to crave an audience with the general.

He found Caesar feeding his goat, while behind him stood the Centurion-Capricorn, holding a fold of his toga discreetly over his nose.

'What is it, soldier?' said the general.

'O great Caesar!' said Oleaginus in his oiliest

7

voice. 'I come with a request from all my fellow legionaries.'

'A request? What about?'

'About that most beautiful of creatures, Your Excellency's goat.'

'What about it?'

'O great Caesar!' said Oleaginus. 'If only this noble animal could lead us into battle! How the sight of it, at the head of the army, would inspire every man behind it, while at the same time striking terror into the hearts of Your Excellency's foes!'

'D'you really think so?' said Caesar.

'Truly, O great Caesar!' replied Oleaginus in a choking voice, his eyes streaming, for the stench of the billy goat in the confined space of the tent was overpowering.

Ye Gods! thought Caesar, observing the legionary's tears. The poor fellow's overcome with emotion. Already my men have come to think of my goat as a mascot. With him to lead them, they'll fight like lions!

So it was that when Caesar's army struck camp next morning to continue the southward march, the north wind still at their backs, the two leading figures in the long column of soldiers were the Centurion-Capricorn and the goat.

When at long last the two opposing armies met, they would have seemed to an observer to be equally matched. On either side were three legions, each of 3,000 men. Within each legion were ten cohorts, each of 300 men. Within each cohort were three centuries, each of 100 men.

But it was an ill wind that blew in the faces of Pompey's army that day, for it carried upon it a thick, choking, acrid smell, before which Pompey's leading troops began first to falter and then to turn away in panic, rank after rank pushing and shoving back through their fellows in an effort to escape that ghastly miasma, until at last the whole army turned tail in a wild stampede.

The history books may tell you that Caesar defeated Pompey in the civil war between those two generals.

Rubbish!

Pompey and his legions were routed by Julius Caesar's goat.

★

With the goat at the head of his army, Caesar was invincible. Sometimes he wondered why it was that his goat seemed to be so powerful a weapon, and occasionally he asked his senior officers for their opinion on the matter.

They of course, fearing for their lives, could not mention the dreadful smell, of which Caesar, had they known it, was quite unaware. So they all agreed to say that they thought the goat must have magic properties, against which no foe could stand. Sometimes in their enthusiasm they would overdo their praise of the animal, so that Julius Caesar had to remind them that, though his goat (and its Centurion-Capricorn) might be leading the legions into battle, it was he, Caesar, who was the real leader.

'Wane-ee, weed-ee, week-ee,' he said, quite a few times after a victory (for that is how modern scholars believe the words '*Veni, vidi, vici*' were pronounced by the ancient Romans – words which meant '*I* came, *I* saw, *I* conquered').

In fact he was reminding his officers that the credit for the victory was his, not the goat's.

But behind his back, they, knowing the reason

for the animal's awful smell, joked that what the goat would say was, 'Wane-ee, weed-ee, wee-wee.'

The goat was not only of value on the field of battle. Caesar found another use for it. Discipline in the Roman army was very strict, and punishments ranged from ten strokes of the *Felis nonecauda* (which, loosely translated, means Cat-o'-nine-tails) to as many as 100. More serious misconduct was punishable by death, usually by decapitation, though officers committing such crimes were required to fall upon their own swords.

None of these penalties was much fun (certainly not for the guilty party), but one day something took place that cheered things up a bit.

It so happened that one of Caesar's commanders wanted a message taken to the general, and who should volunteer to carry it but that little creep Oleaginus. As before, he found Caesar in his tent, at his side the goat, in the background the Centurion-Capricorn (once a strong and healthy man but now pale and thin through loss of appetite). Oleaginus delivered the message, bowed low in his smarmy way, and turned to leave the tent.

Something about the rear view of the little legionary sparked off a sudden reaction in the brain of the goat and it charged across the floor of the tent, head down, so that its great curved horns struck Oleaginus squarely on his backside, and he went flying out through the tent-flap.

Once the general and his Centurion-Capricorn and his bodyguard and everyone else nearby had stopped laughing, it occurred to Caesar that here was an excellent form of punishment for minor offences, such as improperly shined sandals or poorly polished shields, offences that didn't really merit a beating with the *Felis nonecauda*. It would be much more fun for everyone (except the victim) to order one butt from Caesar's goat.

News of this soon spread through the legions, and from then on it was remarkable to see, at punishment parades, just how many offenders were sent by their centurions to receive this novel comeuppance. For onlookers it was great entertainment, and for Caesar's goat it was a useful form of exercise.

The miscreant was made to stand with his back to the goat, his tunic hitched up to expose his bottom. Then, at the command 'Forward!' (a Celtic word that Caesar had learned during his campaigns in Britain in 55 and 54 BC), the Centurion-Capricorn would release the goat.

Before long this novel punishment became a recognized sport, and measurements began to be kept of the distance through which the goat could knock a wrongdoer. Bets were laid, and, however badly bruised, it was a proud man who held the current All-Comers' Long Butt record.

Caesar was extremely pleased with his goat and he issued another edict, forbidding anyone else to own such an animal.

'Just as there is only one man called Julius Caesar,' he said to the commanders of his three legions, 'so there will only ever be one goat in Caesar's army.'

'Called what, O great Caesar?' someone said.

'Hm. Yes. Come to think of it,' said Caesar,

'it really ought to have a name. Can anyone suggest a suitable one?'

The commanders hesitated. They all knew the sort of names they'd like to call the goat, such as 'Ponger' or 'Niffy' or 'Stinkbomb'. But none of them wanted to risk being told to fall upon his sword. So they suggested complimentary names like 'Braveheart' and 'Stronghorn' and 'Conqueror'. But Caesar didn't seem to like any of them.

'I can see I'll have to choose a name myself,' he said.

He thought for a while, and then suddenly he smote himself upon the brow and smiled broadly.

'*Habeo solutionem!*' he cried (which, loosely translated, means 'I've got it!').

'What, O great Caesar?' they asked.

'Well, what's yellow and greasy and you spread it on your bread?' he asked.

'Butter,' they replied.

'And what does this goat do?'

Resisting, one and all, the desire to say, 'Stink!' they replied, 'Butt.'

'Well, then,' said Caesar, 'that's it. It's name is Butter.'

The commanders looked at one another.

'Oh,' they said.

Then they looked at Caesar and saw that he thought this was the greatest of jokes.

'Oh, yes!' they all said hastily. 'Oh, ha ha ha! Oh, HA HA HA HA!'

In the winter of 48/47 BC, Julius Caesar took a holiday. He needed a rest from constant battles and decided to go to Egypt, for a variety of reasons.

The Egyptians, he had heard, were well disposed towards goats, so he thought Butter would like it. He wanted to see the Pyramids and the Sphinx, monuments that were far, far older than anything Rome had to offer, and also to see the Nile, the greatest river in the known world. But principally (though he didn't let on about this) he wanted to have a look at Cleopatra, Queen of Egypt, reputedly the most beautiful woman of all time.

So Caesar set sail for Alexandria, accompanied

by Butter and the Centurion-Capricorn, and the bodyguard, and a couple of cohorts just to be on the safe side.

Little did he know that Cleopatra, like him, had problems relating to the nose. His was large and Roman and a bit bent, hers was small and straight and pretty. He, as we know, had absolutely no sense of smell, she an excellent one.

But it was what she liked to smell, and to smell of, that was the trouble.

Cleopatra, you see, had no use for sweet-smelling salves and unguents and perfumes, and the kind of fragrant scents that women usually like to put upon themselves. She preferred really strong, powerful malodours from which most people would run a mile.

Of all the bad smells in the world, the worst is said to be that of Siberian wolf's urine, and Cleopatra had supplies of this regularly imported to use as her own personal scent.

It was therefore not surprising that there was a great lack of suitors for the (very smelly) hand of this so beautiful Queen, and Cleopatra, receiving news of the impending arrival of Julius Caesar, nursed a hope that this eminent Roman soldier might be different from the dandified gentlemen of her court, who all smelt so horribly clean.

I do hope he doesn't wash, she said to herself. I long for a man with really fruity body odour. Little did she guess what treats were in store for her.

When Caesar's fleet docked at Alexandria, the first thing he did was to send a message to Queen Cleopatra, announcing his arrival and requesting the favour of an audience. This being granted, Caesar stepped ashore and set out for Cleopatra's palace.

He took his bodyguard with him, but left the goat behind in the care of the Centurion-Capricorn. Who could tell, Butter might take a dislike to the Egyptian Queen as he had to Oleaginus. Just imagine! Once within the palace, Caesar was welcomed by the Comptroller of the Queen's Household, who somehow managed by a supreme effort of will to disguise his disgust at the rank effluvium surrounding this distinguished visitor (for of course Caesar, through constant association with his goat, smelt just as bad as it did, if not worse).

'Greetings, O Caesar!' gasped the Comptroller, mopping his eyes. 'Pray follow me to Her Majesty's boudoir, for it is her wish that you and she meet alone,' and, having led the way along a maze of corridors, he stopped at a gilded door, opened it, ushered Caesar in and closed the door again behind the general.

There was thus no witness of that first meeting between Caesar and Cleopatra, but there was equally no doubt of the immediate effect of the one upon the other.

Caesar saw before him a vision of incomparable loveliness, elegantly dressed in rich silks, a jewelled crown upon her dark hair.

He heard the music of her husky voice as she greeted him.

He felt, as he took her hand and bowed over it to kiss it, the velvety softness of her skin.

But he knew nothing at all of the smell of that skin, liberally drenched as it was in Siberian wolf's urine.

By Jupiter! he thought. What a woman!

Cleopatra saw before her the short, stocky figure (for Julius Caesar was but three cubits tall – about five foot, that's to say) of a balding middle-aged man with a broken nose.

Nothing much to look at, she thought, but by Osiris and Isis, he stinks to high heaven! What a whiff, what a pong. It's enough to knock you down! How can I resist such a foul-smelling man?

And so they fell in love, Caesar at first sight, Cleopatra at first sniff.

When Cleopatra first came to meet Julius Caesar's goat, the Centurion-Capricorn had the animal on a collar and chain, with strict instructions to hang on tight. Caesar didn't want to risk any unfortunate incident.

In fact, however, Butter was well behaved on first introduction to the Queen. He merely stood with raised head, his rubbery lips curled back, his yellow eyes half closed, and sniffed appreciatively at the strange strong scent of the lady.

As for Cleopatra, she was delighted. By the great King Cheops! she said to herself. This Julius Caesar even has his own matching accessory, a designer goat that smells exactly as he does! What a man!

'Do you like him, Clee?' asked Caesar (already they had pet names for each other).

'Oh yes, Jujube!' cried Cleopatra. 'I just love the way he smells!'

'And how does he smell, would you say?' asked Caesar.

'Like you.'

'And how do I smell, would you say?'

'Gorgeous!' said the Queen of Egypt. 'Almost as gorgeous as me. You do like the way I smell, don't you, Jujube?'

Caesar sniffed deeply. Can't smell a damned thing, he thought, but I mustn't let on.

'Wonderful, Clee,' he said. 'Wonderful.'

At the end of his Egyptian holiday, Caesar set sail for Italy, accompanied by his goat, the Centurion-Capricorn, the bodyguard, the two cohorts and, you won't be surprised to hear, Cleopatra.

So that now it was the wretched people of Rome who had to put up with the awful combined stinks of Caesar, his goat and his ladylove.

One look (from a distance) at Cleopatra and the Romans said to one another, 'She's beautiful!'

One sniff at her (close up) and they couldn't wait to be out of range, for a breath of fresh air and to say to one another, 'By Jupiter! What a pong! How can Caesar stand that?'

'How can she stand the smell of him, for that matter?'

'To say nothing of that goat!'

'She's the worst, by a league!'

'She never washes, they say!'

'Never?'

'No, and never takes a bath!'

This last, the Romans found out a little later, was not strictly true. Cleopatra did indeed not wash. She considered that her imported Siberian scent was much too costly to be regularly rinsed away. But once a month, at the full moon, she took a bath.

She had not been in Rome many days before she said to Caesar, 'By the way, Jujube, in a couple of weeks' time the moon will be full and I shall be having my bath. Get it all fixed up for me, will you?'

'No problem, Clee,' said Caesar. 'I have a fine bath-house in my mansion. The pool in it holds 100 gallons of water. I'll have it heated to whatever temperature you wish. They won't need two weeks' notice.'

'They will,' said Cleopatra. 'The Queen of Egypt does not bathe in water.'

'Oh,' said Caesar. 'Well, what do you bathe in?'

'Milk.'

'Cows' milk?'

'No, asses' milk.'

'Oh,' said Caesar. 'I see,' he said (though he didn't). 'Still, that won't take two weeks. I'll issue an edict straight away, ordering every she-ass in Rome and district that is presently suckling a foal to be rounded up and milked. We should be able to get 100 gallons of fresh asses' milk in a couple of days.'

'Oh, Jujube!' said Cleopatra. 'Don't be such a donkey! I don't want fresh asses' milk. It's got to have time to go sour, to go off, to curdle, to get really fruity. That's the way I like it.'

'Oh,' said Caesar. 'I see,' he said (though he

didn't). Perhaps that way it's good for her skin, he thought.

He could not know that Cleopatra had long ago discovered that though her imported Siberian scent might be supposed – by other people – to be the worst smell in the world, it could be made even more awful – more lovely to her – if it was applied over a coating of really sour asses' milk.

Thus, when she emerged from her monthly bath, she would not allow her handmaidens to dry her. Instead they must immediately spray her milk-soaked skin with Siberian wolf's urine.

The edict which Caesar now issued required all those who could supply asses' milk to bring their donkeys to the Colosseum. The Romans loved a good spectacle (usually of people killing one another or being killed by wild beasts like lions), but Caesar thought that an ass-milking competition might be a nice change and rather fun, and could attract a good crowd.

Accordingly, he offered two prizes of money. The *denarius* was the chief Roman silver coin (oddly enough, each was worth ten smaller coins called *asses*), and Caesar offered 100 *denarii* for the man who milked his donkey quickest, and another 100 for the owner of the donkey that gave the most milk.

On the day, not surprisingly, the donkey mares were upset at being taken to a strange place, to be milked by hand instead of suckling their foals, in front of a great crowd of cheering onlookers. Being donkeys, they behaved as stubbornly and as awkwardly as possible, kicking the milk pails over, kicking the milkers and biting them, and escaping from their handlers to gallop round the Colosseum, kicking and biting other donkeys as they went.

But the crowd loved it, and the prizes were awarded, and at last 100 gallons of asses' milk were collected and taken to Caesar's mansion and poured into the square stone pool in his bath-house.

The weather in Rome was very hot that summer, and the milk began to go off very quickly, so that by the time of the full moon the pong in Caesar's bath-house was unbearable to everyone (except Caesar, who couldn't smell it, and Cleopatra, who thought it heavenly).

The Centurion-Capricorn – who, after all, had to put up with more day-to-day stink than anyone else – summed up the general feeling. '*Dum spiro, spero,*' he said (which, loosely translated, means 'As long as I'm still breathing, there's hope').

There was, however, something else happening during those two weeks while the asses' milk was going bad. Butter was beginning to suffer from two of the seven deadly sins.

The first was envy. To begin with, Julius Caesar's goat had not thought much about this new woman that had come into his master's life. But day by day he became increasingly jealous of the Queen of Egypt.

Time was when Caesar spent all his spare moments with his goat. Now he spent them all with Cleopatra. Butter did not like this state of affairs at all. Which led him to the second deadly sin – anger.

By the time that the moon was full, on the day in fact when Cleopatra was to take her bath, Butter's feelings towards her were as hostile as they could possibly be.

In the bath-house, the scene was set.

Cleopatra stood at the edge of the pool full of foul-smelling, curdled asses' milk. Around her were gathered her handmaidens, waiting to remove her robes and then to assist her as she walked down the steps into the pool.

The only other person in the bath-house was Julius Caesar, who thought it would be fun to stand behind a pillar and play Peeping Tom.

Just at that moment Butter came in, trailing a length of rope. The Centurion-Capricorn had tied him up (on Caesar's orders), but the goat had chewed through the tether.

Now, at the precise moment when the hand-maidens had removed the Queen's robes and she had taken her first step into the pool, Julius Caesar's goat set eyes on the rear view of his master's new favourite.

Such was the force with which Butter's horns struck the royal bottom that Cleopatra was cata-pulted far out into the deep end, and disappeared under the horrid mess of clotted curds and watery whey, to surface again, spluttering and gasping, while the handmaidens ran wildly about, in their hands the royal clothing, while one of them carried a great glass phial filled ready with Siberian wolf's urine.

Then to the ears of the furious Queen there came, from behind a pillar, the sound of someone giggling, and the giggle became a chuckle, and the chuckle became a gale of laughter as Julius Caesar stepped forth, rocking about in hysterical mirth at the sight before his streaming eyes.

'Oh, Clee!' he gasped. 'You've easily beaten the All-Comers' Long Butt record!'

So long and loudly did he roar that all the members of his household, and even passers-by from the street, came running to see what the joke was: and they too all burst into loud guffaws at the sight of the smelly Queen floundering furiously about in a sea of stinking asses' milk.

Caesar should have known better. No one likes to be laughed at in public, and no one likes it less than a queen.

Cleopatra caught the next boat back to Alexandria.

Everyone (except the general) was heartily glad to see the back of the Queen of Egypt. Butter had been particularly pleased to see the back of her.

Had she stayed, who can tell how different the future might have been for Julius Caesar, but as it was, he too now began to suffer from another of the seven deadly sins – pride.

For some time he had been admired by the people and by the soldiery, as victorious generals commonly are. Winning every battle is a sure way to popularity, even if you smell as bad as, thanks to his goat, Caesar did. More, again thanks to the goat, all these battles were won with hardly any casualties amongst Caesar's legionaries, for the enemy always ran away from the terrible smell borne towards them on the wind. No wonder then that the general became increasingly pleased with himself, and during the years 46 and 45 BC (when he easily defeated the remnants of Pompey's armies) he declared himself the dictator of the Roman Empire.

Supreme power was his, riches were his,

everyone scurried to do his slightest bidding. The world, it seemed, was his oyster.

Like many dictators, however, he was lonely. Everyone kowtowed to him but nobody really liked him. Except his goat.

He had no one to talk to, again except his goat, so he took to having long chats to it.

'Wouldn't Mater and Pater be amazed if they could see me now, Butter?' he would say. 'Look at it this way. The Roman Empire is the most powerful force in the whole world. I am the most powerful man in the Roman Empire. Ergo, I am the most powerful man in the world! *Quod erat demonstrandum!*'

On the minus side, Caesar, like all dictators, had his enemies.

In the Senate, the governing body of ancient Rome, there were a number of men who viewed Julius Caesar's overweening pride with dismay. These republican senators suspected that Caesar, not content with being dictator, had his eye on an even higher position: to become, in fact, the monarch of all he surveyed, to be Emperor.

Of these senators, two in particular were 100 *per centum* anti-Caesar.

One of them was none other than that very Brutus who had, more than forty years ago, clobbered Caesar's sense of smell with that overhead kick.

The other, Cassius by name, had also been at North Rome Primary School at the same time, with a reputation for twisting smaller boys' arms or stamping on their toes.

Now they made a fine pair, at one in their jealousy of Caesar and their desire to take him down a peg.

'He's become a proper bighead,' said Brutus.

'Too big for his boots as well,' said Cassius.

'He must be removed.'

'Removed? You mean . . .'

'No, no,' said Brutus. 'Not what you're thinking, Cassius. For that we would pay with our lives. No, there must be some way to limit his powers.'

'I wish we could limit the smell of the fellow,' said Cassius. 'Him and his goat.'

But in fact it was Julius Caesar's goat who, all

unknowingly, decided the fate of his master.

It happened like this.

One fine day Caesar was out for a walk with Butter. He had given the Centurion–Capricorn the day off, for the goat walked to heel like a well-trained dog, and so they were alone (or so it appeared, though of course members of Caesar's bodyguard were discreetly walking nearby, trying to look like ordinary citizens and at the same time trying to keep upwind of the goat).

As the dictator and his pet walked by the banks of the River Tiber, who should they come upon, by chance, but Brutus and Cassius, sitting on a bench (just feeding the ducks, it seemed, though actually they were busy trying to plot the dictator's downfall).

They looked up, saw Caesar and got to their feet.

'*Salve!*' they cried (which, loosely translated, means 'Hi, there!').

Caesar frowned. He had never liked these two, neither Brutus, for obvious reasons connected with his nose, nor Cassius, who had twisted his arms and stood on his toes.

'We're not in the playground at North Rome Primary now,' he said in his most imperious voice. 'You will kindly address me in the proper manner.'

Brutus and Cassius, half a cubit taller than the dictator, looked down at him. They looked round, and saw the bodyguard closing quietly in. They looked at one another, and then they forced themselves to offer the proper greeting.

'*Salve*, O great Caesar!' they said.

'That's better,' said Caesar. 'What are you doing here anyway?'

'Just feeding the ducks,' they said, and they turned to face the river, pointing to the quacking birds.

Butter regarded their senatorial backsides. Intuitively he knew that his master did not like these men, so, loyally, neither did he. He put his head down and took a run at Brutus and knocked him over the bank and down into the Tiber. Then he did the same to Cassius. As had happened in the case of Cleopatra and her bath, Caesar thought this one heck of a joke, and so, I'm sorry to say, did his bodyguard, who all came running, to laugh their heads off at the sight of the two senators sploshing about in the murky water.

With great difficulty, because of their water-logged togas, Brutus and Cassius somehow struggled to the bank — the far bank, as far as they could from the guffawing spectators.

As they crawled out, covered in various bits of muck, Brutus said once more to Cassius, 'He must be removed.'

In return, Cassius, as before, said, 'Removed? You mean . . .'

'Yes,' said Brutus. 'This time I do mean exactly what you're thinking,' and then, as one man, they turned their thumbs down.

There was only one place to do the deed, they decided later, and that was in the senate-house, for the simple reason that only senators were allowed to enter it. Thus Caesar's bodyguard would not be able to protect him.

Brutus and Cassius called a secret meeting of a number of hard-faced republicans — Casca, Metellus and Cinna among them — who had long wanted to bring down Caesar, and could now be persuaded to help in getting rid of him for ever.

By a strange chance, they settled upon the Ides of March 44 BC – the forty-sixth anniversary of that playground incident – as the day for the deed.

When, that morning, Caesar walked into the senate-house, leaving his bodyguard outside, the conspirators thronged around him with many cries of '*Salve*, O great Caesar!', all wearing broad smiles as though delighted to see him, and pressing closer and closer to the dictator. Then they all drew their swords and plunged them into Caesar's body.

One face amongst those of the assassins swam before the victim's failing sight, and once more he cried, '*Et tu, Brute!*'

Then he uttered his last words, '*Caesar moriturus est!*' (which, precisely translated, means 'Caesar is about to die!') and he did.

Meanwhile, back at Caesar's mansion, Butter, by that strange sixth sense that some animals have, had become worried about his master. Some instinct told him that all was not well, and once more he chewed through his tether, and set off through the streets of Rome, following the trail until he came to the senate-house.

By the time the goat reached the scene of the murder, all the conspirators had fled except Brutus and Cassius, who still stood facing one another on either side of Caesar's body, their bloodstained swords upraised, looking down with evil satisfaction at the corpse.

This was what Butter saw as he bounded into the senate-house.

There, directly before him, was one of those senatorial bottoms with which he had dealt so effectively on the banks of the Tiber. He hit it at full speed (it was Brutus's) and the impact hurled the man forward into Cassius. Both the murderers fell dead across the body of their victim.

Afterwards, it was the general opinion that Brutus and Cassius, appalled at the deed they had done, had decided, like true Roman gentlemen, to fall upon their swords. In fact, they had fallen upon each other's.

As for Butter, he bent his great horned head above the body of his master and uttered one low groan of farewell. Then he turned and left the senate-house.

If you like happy endings, then I'm afraid the story of Julius Caesar did not have one.

But on the other hand, the story of Julius Caesar's goat did. Once the fuss over the dictator's assassination had died down and he had been buried with full military honours, and the rest of the conspirators had dutifully fallen upon their own swords, the Senate met to discuss how they could best commemorate the life of the late, great general.

One of the senators suggested that they should confer honours upon his beloved pet.

'Caesar would have liked that,' he said. 'Thumbs up, everyone who approves the idea,' and the motion was carried unanimously.

At first they considered making Butter a senator, until they realized that the goat would then have access to the senate-house, stink and all.

Then they decided to make Julius Caesar's goat

a Proconsul, namely a kind of Roman magistrate with authority outside the city.

'Proconsul of what?' someone asked.

'Of the Seven Hills,' someone else suggested, for Rome was and still is surrounded by seven hills.

It may not be so nowadays, but in 44 BC great flocks of wild goats roamed these hills, and Butter, the senators said to one another, would have a high old time.

And so he did. Being bigger and stronger and a better butter than all the other billy goats, he beat them up and pinched their wives and became the father of umpteen children.

Nor was he the only one to benefit from his newfound freedom, for now there was no further need for the services of his minder, the Centurion-Capricorn. He reverted to plain centurion and lost his extra one *denarius per diem*, but a fat lot he cared. At last he was free of that ghastly pong that, over the last five years, had destroyed his appetite and marred his enjoyment of life, and the colour came back into his pale cheeks and he began to put on weight.

Butter the Proconsul roamed the Seven Hills of Rome in perfect freedom and contentment, until he died peacefully in his sleep in 36 BC. He was then fifteen years old (a ripe old age for a ripe old goat) and the senators held a meeting to decide what should be done with his body.

'Shall we cremate him?' said somebody. 'Build a huge funeral pyre and stick him on it and set fire to it?'

'Or shall we bury him,' said someone else, 'with the honour due to a Proconsul of course, and a fine headstone above his grave?'

'No,' said another senator. 'Tell you what. Let's stuff him.'

So they engaged the services of the leading taxidermist of the day, who made a superb job of it, and they placed the finished article in the Temple of Jupiter, on the Capitoline Hill.

The great stuffed goat became one of the best-loved sights of the Eternal City, and maters and paters took their kids to see him, himself the father of countless kids.

There he stood in the Capitol, his fine bearded head raised, his great horns thrown back so as almost to touch the (smell-free) ginger hair of his withers, his yellow (glass) eyes surveying the city below.

Each year, on the fifteenth – the Ides – March, a teacher would bring a class from North Rome Primary up to the Capitol and, pointing at the proud figure of Butter, Proconsul of the Seven Hills, would say, 'Now, children, who is this?'

Then loudly, all the children cried:

'IT'S JULIUS CAESAR'S GOAT!!'

Gillian Cross

THE CLOAK THAT I LEFT WITH CARPUS

Italy and Turkey, AD 65

I chose this time and place because of the cloak. I wanted to write a story that was linked with the man who owned it.

In the eleventh year of the Emperor Nero, Helena was ten years old. And her mother died.

The Ladies (her mother's dear friends) cried until their pretty eyes were red. Then they came and told Helena to pack her clothes.

'You must go to your uncle Carpus,' they said. 'In Troas.'

Troas sounded foreign and far away. Helena was helpless with misery. She begged to stay in her mother's villa, with its elegant murals and its mosaic floor, but the Ladies laughed like a flock of singing birds.

'It's not your mother's villa!' they said. 'Soon, someone else will move in, and you must be gone before she comes.'

Helena begged and sulked, but the Ladies just smiled and patted their scented hair.

'You must go to Carpus,' they said. 'He'll teach you to be good. He thinks being good is *very* important.'

One of them twisted her painted face into a heavy frown and glared at the others. They opened their eyes wide and backed away, pretending to be terrified.

Helena imagined a cold, stern uncle. A monster of strictness. She stopped sulking and stamping and began to freeze into herself.

Two weeks after her mother's death, the Ladies came for the last time. They took Helena and her bundle down to Puteoli, to the harbour, and haggled with an ugly sea captain, who laughed at their jokes and patted their pretty faces. Helena stood by, still and quiet, looking up at his bearded face.

When the Ladies had given her food for the voyage and gone fluttering back to Rome, it seemed best to go on being still and quiet. Clutching her bundle of clothes, Helena curled up in a corner of the deck.

At first, the sailors spoke to her as they passed, but she turned her head away. And once they set sail, and the ship began to pitch, she was too sick to answer anyway. They began to ignore her, and she sank into silence. It was easier not to speak.

For weeks they sailed east. As the sea grew wilder, she heard the sailors muttering that it was bad luck to sail with a dumb girl on board. But the words floated past, without touching her. The silence was a hard shell now, cutting her off from people's voices.

They reached Troas on a grey, dark day, with wind whipping the sea into breakers. The captain was anxious to sail on to Sidon and he had no time to waste on Helena. Leading her down on to the quay, he snatched at the first urchin he saw.

'Do you know Carpus?' he yelled, above the wind.

The boy's eyes flickered cunningly and he held out a hand. Even Helena, wrapped in her silence, knew that he wanted money. With stiff fingers, she untied her bundle and took out one of the coins the Ladies had given her.

'There's another when you take her to Carpus!' the captain shouted. Then he patted Helena's shoulder.

She saw, with some remote, cold part of herself, that he was being kind, and she wanted to say, *Don't send me to Carpus! Take me with you!* But she couldn't speak the words. The captain went away, leaving her to follow the boy.

Carpus's house was not like the villa where her mother had lived. That was big and scented, with beautiful gardens and steaming kitchens. Carpus's house was a small building in a street of shops. When the boy stopped outside, Helena caught at his sleeve, wanting him to stay with her. But he pulled away, holding out a hand for his second coin. When she took it out, he snatched it and ran off, leaving her on her own. Lowering her head, she knocked on the rough, wooden door.

It creaked open. In front of her, she saw a huge pair of feet. Hairy, like a bear's. Trembling, she held out a hand, with her mother's ring pushed clumsily on to the thumb.

'Is she dead, then?' said a deep, gruff voice. 'My sister?'

This was Carpus? For an instant, Helena looked up, glimpsing massive shoulders and a heavy, lined face. Then, as he held his arms out to her, she backed away. Pointing at her mouth, she shook her head, to make him understand that she wouldn't speak.

'Come inside,' he said.

Helena watched his feet move away and she followed, down a narrow passage into a room where a woman was sitting. As the woman looked round, Helena lowered her head again.

'I think this is my sister's daughter,' Carpus said. 'But she doesn't speak.'

Behind her barrier of silence, Helena waited for questions. The Ladies would have asked a hundred questions, trying to trick her into talking. But there was nothing. Only a moment of stillness. Then the woman stood up.

'Come,' she said gently. 'I can see you're not ready for strangers. I'll find you some food and a place to sleep.'

She picked up Helena's box and beckoned her on down the passage, to a small room at the back of the house.

'Here you can sleep,' she said. 'No one will disturb you. Settle yourself while I fetch some food.'

She brought a bowl of beans and some flat bread. Then she said good night, hovering in the doorway for a moment. Helena shrank back against the wall, with a little dip of her head for thanks.

'God bless you, my dear,' the woman said as she went out.

Helena had no idea which god she meant. She had no idea which god would bless her in this strange place. But she was glad she had escaped from her huge, fearsome uncle.

When she had eaten the beans and bread, she walked slowly round the room, feeling the walls with her hands. It was small and square, with places for storing cooking pots and firewood. In one corner was a bag of dried beans, and in another was a straw mattress with a couple of coverlets folded on top of it.

At the far end were two dark shelves. One held books and scrolls. On the other was a bundle of thick, dark cloth. She picked up a corner of the cloth and rubbed it between her fingers.

It was quite different from her mother's elegant clothes. It felt rough, like goat's hair, and the harshness made her nerve ends tingle. She rubbed it again.

Nothing had seemed as real as that since her mother died.

She tugged the cloth off the shelf and unfolded it. It was a big, circular cloak, with an opening in the centre. Pulling it over her head, she lay down on the mattress and rolled over, winding her whole body into the cloak. She fell asleep feeling its roughness against her face.

In the morning, the woman came again. When she saw the cloak, she stopped in the doorway for a moment and then came across the room.

'There are better covers,' she said quickly. 'Please –'

She reached for the goat's-hair cloak, but before she could lay a finger on it Helena snatched it away and cowered back, scowling. The woman hesitated and then made a gentle movement with her hand.

'All right,' she said. 'Keep it for now. Will you come and eat?'

Roughly, Helena shook her head, curling up inside the big black cloak.

She stayed like that for three days. The woman came in with food, or simply to talk, and gradually Helena understood that her name was Lalage and that she was Carpus's wife.

She was not like the Ladies, who would have gossiped over Helena's head, opening her box and turning over her belongings. Lalage came alone and sometimes she did not even speak. She sat quietly beside the cloak, with Helena wrapped inside it, sewing or preparing vegetables.

On the fourth day, she came to say that everyone in the house was going out. 'We are going to meet the brothers and sisters. Will you come?'

Whose brothers and sisters? Helena imagined dozens of men and women, all with Carpus's heavy bear-face. She shook her head and shrank away. It was better to stay inside the room, where Carpus didn't come.

But when everyone had gone, she stood up slowly and stiffly. Lifting the cloak in front of her, she walked through the house, running her hands over the walls and opening chests to see what was inside.

For the first time, she found her uncle's work-room, and discovered that he was a potter. And she went into the kitchen, where she had heard Lalage laughing and talking with the other women.

By the fire was a big cooking pot, full of thick lentil stew. Helena looked at it, imagining how her mother's face would have twisted at the coarse food. Her mother had held feasts of the best food in Rome, although she hardly ate a morsel herself, even when rich men coaxed her with honey cakes and lark's tongues.

But when Helena dipped a finger into the stew and tasted it, it was delicious. She wanted to eat more, but she did not dare to, in case Carpus came back and caught her stealing his food.

She padded back to the storeroom in her bare feet, pulling the black cloak round her. When the others came back, she was curled in her corner again, with the cloak over her face.

The strangest thing about the house did not strike her until the next afternoon. She was sitting up on her mattress, watching Lalage make patterns on an unfired pot. There had been a pot of just that shape in the little shrine in her mother's house. Remembering it, Helena realized that there was no shrine to the gods. Not anywhere in the house. She sat up straighter and for a moment a question trembled on the edge of her tongue.

Then Lalage looked up, and she knew that she could not break her silence. Anyway, whatever gods there were, they had forgotten her.

Next time the household went to meet the mysterious brothers and sisters, Lalage was more eager for Helena to come. She brought a small cloak, embroidered in red and green, and held it out for Helena to try.

Helena put out a hand to touch it. She imagined draping it over her shoulders and walking out of the house and along the street. For a moment she longed to go. Then she thought of Carpus and she shrank back into the black cloak, shaking her head.

This time, as soon as everyone had left, she got up and went to sit by the fire in the kitchen. There was a loaf of flat bread by the cooking pots and she picked at one edge of it, rolling the bread into pellets and chewing them. Outside the wind was beating at the walls of the house, but it was warm by the fire and she slid out of the cloak, letting it fall at her feet.

It began to rain, drumming loudly on the roof and the shutters. At first, she didn't hear the other sound. But it went on and on until she noticed it, a faint, insistent tapping beneath the noise of the rain. Leaving her seat by the fire, she went down the passage to the door, putting her eye to a crack to see who was standing outside.

A little boy was leaning against the door. His

face was pale and he was shivering so hard that he could barely stay upright. His ragged clothes were soaked through, and his feet were dirty and sore.

Once, Helena had seen a boy like that at the door of her mother's house. The Ladies had cooed over him and pressed coins and honey cakes into his shrivelled hand. She tapped on the door and the boy's head turned.

His eyes were dark and his face had shrunk into hollows. Helena wanted to signal to him, to indicate that she would bring him something, but the door was between them and he couldn't see her. He looked at the door for a moment and then gave up, turning his head away listlessly. Sinking into icy silence. Helena saw him slide down the door and settle himself on the ground, too exhausted to avoid the puddles.

She turned and ran back down the passage to the little storeroom. Unwrapping her bundle, she felt for the last of the Ladies' coins. Then, clutching them in her hand, she flew back to the door, meaning to post them through the crack.

But when she peered out again, she saw the

boy sitting on the wet ground, with his knees up and his head drooped on to them. Looking down at the coins she was holding – all the money she had in the world – she saw that they were not enough. If she gave them to him, he would still be lost and alone.

Putting her shoulder under the bar that closed the door, she lifted it up and let the door swing wide. Without even lifting his head, the boy put a hand out for the money.

Helena bent down and put the coins into his hand. Then, before he could move away, she slipped her fingers round his wrist and pulled. He blinked, looking blank and stupid.

She knew the Ladies would have lost patience with him then and pushed him away. But she understood. He had gone so far into the cold silence that he could not focus on her. She tugged harder at his hand and, slowly, he uncoiled and stood up. He was older than she had thought, seven or eight maybe, but very thin and weak. Tugging with both hands, she pulled him after her through the passage and into the kitchen.

He was shivering harder now. She made him

sit by the fire, but even then he did not stop. Helena looked at the bread and the pot full of lentils, and she thought of Carpus and his huge, terrifying face.

Then she looked at the boy and saw that he had to eat.

Taking a bowl, she filled it with lentils scooped recklessly from the pot. She broke off a piece of bread and held out the bread and the bowl to the boy. But he stared at them with empty eyes, as if they didn't mean anything.

Helena looked round the kitchen for a spoon. Instead, she saw the black cloak lying on the floor. Setting the bowl down on the hearth, she picked up a corner of the cloak and held it to the boy's face. Very gently, she rubbed it against his cheek, letting him feel the roughness of the goat's hair.

He blinked again and looked at her properly, for the first time. Distantly, like someone peering through icy, silent mists. For a second, Helena was afraid of twittering uselessly, like the Ladies, and frightening him into silence for ever.

Then she thought of Lalage. She smiled and

rubbed the cloth gently against his cheek again, lifting the rest of the cloak to wrap it round him. Round and round, until he had almost disappeared in the thick black folds. Then she dipped the bread into the lentils.

When she held it out, his thin mouth fell open and he began to suck at it. Some of the lentils slid down his chin on to the cloak, but Helena ignored those and dipped the bread again, moving quietly and slowly. Like Lalage.

It took a long time. For half an hour, he ate lentils from the bread, until at last he shook his head and pushed the bowl away. Helena understood that he had eaten all his shrunken stomach could manage.

And that was when she heard the voices.

'The door's open!' Carpus said.

'Helena!' There was a catch in Lalage's voice. 'Has she gone?'

Beside the fire, the boy looked up, with frightened eyes. Helena patted his shoulder, through the thick cloth, and stood up to wait for Carpus and Lalage.

They did not come alone. There was a crowd

of men and women behind them, looking over their shoulders. Helena knew what they could see. A thin, dirty boy, with traces of stolen lentils round his mouth, and a black cloak spattered with dribbled lentils and stained with mud and dust from the boy's feet.

Carpus walked slowly across the room and stood looking down at the boy. And at the filthy cloak. Then he turned towards the doorway, to a small man in shabby travelling clothes.

'I'm sorry, Timothy,' he said. 'This is Paul's cloak. The one you came for.'

Helena looked at the small man and understood that he had come to take the black cloak away.

Carpus bent over the boy, stretching out a hand, and Helena thought he was going to snatch the cloak. Furiously, she flung herself at him, grabbing his arm to stop him.

'No!' she shouted.

Her voice was rough and harsh, because she had not spoken for so long, and she was terrified, but she forced out more words.

'He can't take the cloak! The boy needs it!'

Carpus stopped, looking at the boy. Then he turned to face Helena. For the first time she looked into his eyes, and she saw that they were as gentle as Lalage's.

'Welcome,' he said, as if she had only just arrived. 'Welcome, dear daughter of my sister.'

Gathering up the folds of his own cloak, he lifted it over his head and held it out to Timothy.

'Will you take this to Paul, in his prison? And tell him that I have two children who cannot spare the other cloak?'

Helena saw Timothy reach out his hands, but she did not hear what he said, because Lalage flew across the room and caught her up, hugging her so hard that she lifted her off the ground.

Carpus picked up the boy, still wrapped in the black cloak. 'Tell Paul I am sorry that I did not keep his cloak safely,' he said.

Timothy smiled. 'You have kept everything safely,' he said. 'And Paul will be very warm in your cloak this winter.'

This is not a true story, but Carpus was a real person. He was one of the first Christians and he was living in Troas in around AD 65. We know because, about then, St Paul wrote from his prison in Rome to his adopted son Timothy: 'When you come, bring the cloak that I left with Carpus at Troas, and my scrolls, especially the parchments.'

Melvin Burgess

AD 1000

People get very excited about dates, but when the time has come and gone the world goes on just the same as before. When the last millennium came, people were much more religious than they are now, and I wanted to do a story about the kind of things they thought then . . . and to poke a little fun at those who take such things a bit too seriously.

The horses, Heavy and John, stood stone still in the rain. Tom thought they looked like big angels watching over them. Gregory, Edwin and the Blessed Judith were struggling to get the big wooden cross upright. It looked from the summit of the hill over the estuary and down to the sea. It was the highest point for miles and the best spot in the kingdom from which to watch God and His angels come down.

Tom was teasing a dog with a stick, making it bark and bark before he finally flung the stick. The horses and people had churned up the hilltop and everyone was covered from head to foot in thick red mud. The Blessed Judith was getting angry.

'Stop teasing that poor mutt,' she hissed, slithering about in the mud under the cross. The cross rose and sank, rose and sank. With a groan, the monks and the woman laid it down flat on its back. They stood about, bent over, hands on knees, panting and gasping with the effort.

'It's a pity they didn't have this trouble getting the first cross up, because then Our Lord would never have been crucified and you'd all be saved this trouble, isn't it, Brothers?' said Tom.

The Blessed Judith and Edwin snorted in amusement. Gregory glared. They were all too exhausted to speak.

The rain started to fall more heavily. Gregory nodded at Tom, as if to say . . . there, you've offended Him. But Edwin winked.

'I just wish we could have had some better weather for Judgement Day,' he said. 'It isn't as if it comes round all that often. You'd have thought there might be a couple of decent days left in the pot.'

Gregory pointed an angry finger at him. 'You . . . blasphemy . . . roast . . .' he groaned hollowly. He was skinny from fasting, and too breathless to get any more out.

'There's nothing blasphemous about having a sense of humour, Brother,' said Edwin.

To prove the point he pushed the Blessed Judith sideways. She stuck up a leg, toppled over and fell with a great slap of her bum into the mud. She grabbed Edwin by the leg and down he went too, so they both ended sitting up to their waists in sludgy water.

They were snorting with laughter, but Gregory was furious. He pointed across the bay, as if he could already see the Heavenly Hosts stepping out of the grey sea mists. 'It'll be hot enough. Just wait a couple of days.' He fixed his beady black eyes on the Blessed Judith. 'Your days will be full of the screaming of scorching souls and the stink of burning flesh,' he hissed.

The Blessed Judith blushed under the mud

and looked down at her feet . . . she was getting nervous about Judgement Day. But Edwin came to her rescue.

'And God never asked you to be so bad-tempered either,' he said. 'I ask you . . . did Jesus ever say, "Just you wait, this is really going to hurt?" Well, then.'

But the Blessed Judith stared across the water, chewing her lip. Gregory leered triumphantly down at the two of them. As far as he was concerned, God would have a few old scores to settle later on.

It was 30 December 999. At midnight tomorrow, the first millennium was coming to an end. The monks of Caderwal Abbey were confidently expecting the End of the World.

'D'you suppose He'll think it a sin that we've failed to get His cross up?' asked Edwin.

Now it was Gregory's turn to worry. He hated to put a foot wrong as far as God was concerned. 'Come on . . . on with it, on with it,' he nagged.

Edwin and the Blessed Judith heaved themselves upright and got back to work. But it was so slippery that in another couple of minutes they were back down, flat on their backs, squirming in the mud.

Tom was delighted. 'Look at you! Look at the pair of you!' he howled.

Edwin and the Blessed Judith turned and smiled at each other, but Gregory stood there, seething with rage.

'It's the end of the world,' he screamed, stamping his sandalled foot into a puddle of thick mud. 'The end of the world! At least you could take it seriously!'

Tom lived in the monastery grounds with the Blessed Judith, his mother. She wasn't at all blessed, really . . . Edwin invented the name for her after the Blessed St Jude, patron saint of lost causes. They were lucky to be allowed to live in the monastery grounds. Tom's father had died in a fishing accident years ago when he was too small to remember, and somehow his uncle Edwin had wangled them a home. The Blessed Judith did the washing and helped look after the orphans. The monks specialized in orphans.

There was a whole school of them attached to the monastery.

The monastery had been busy for weeks now with the millennium celebrations. There had been a fair, which was fun. There had been prayers, music and chanting and endless confessions. The last thing you wanted was to get judged unconfessed, with all your sins still on you. The queues to the confession booths were never less than three hours long these days.

The whole community was going up the hill to get a good view of God and His angels coming down to earth in a blaze of glory. There would be no sight like it, not since the world began. There was going to be a good bonfire, despite Brother Gregory, who said it would be in bad taste to have a fire, what with all the frying that was going to go on later in the evening. But the Abbot didn't see why it was to God's greater glory to be freezing your toes off when the great hour came.

The end of the world meant different things to different people. Some feared it, some welcomed it as a chance to move on to a better place. There were so many opinions that Tom found it difficult to take seriously.

The Abbot was looking forward to it.

'It'll be a grand day,' he kept saying, rubbing his hands together, just as he used to say of feast days. Well, he was the Abbot. He had nothing to worry about.

Uncle Edwin agreed that the whole day would pass off comfortably. 'I don't believe in all this gnashing-of-teeth stuff,' he told Tom. 'Jesus is the lamb, isn't he? No, no . . . He's not the feller to make a big fuss about things . . .'

The likes of Brother Gregory, on the other hand, were positively gloating about the fate of the sinners. He took great pleasure in going into the village and terrorizing the population with tales about hellfire and the tortures the Devil had waiting for them.

The Blessed Judith didn't know what to make of the whole thing. 'Well, they say the afterlife has a lot going for it, so all in all I don't mind so much the world ending, so long as it doesn't hurt too much. It all depends where you get sent, doesn't it?' She bit her lip nervously. Everyone said that God was willing to forgive your sins, but who could be sure? It was no good asking the monks either. 'You've got one lot of them telling you you're going to fry, another lot telling you it'll be like a nice day out . . . I don't know what to make of it,' she said. 'Monks never agree on anything,' she added crossly.

As for Tom . . . well, he was looking forward to the bonfire. The world was so big and wide, he didn't believe for one second that anyone was going to wipe it out, not even God. But he never said anything about that. He was enjoying it all too much.

On the great day the rain stopped at midday as if on cue . . . maybe it was. The ground underfoot was sodden but the air had been washed clean. You could see for miles. The view of the Holy Hosts should be terrific.

Everyone was there, up on the hillside. Some of the older monks had been dragged out on litters. A number of them had been putting off dying for years just for this day. Many of the villagers had been camping since early in the day in order to get the best view. The hillside was sprinkled with trails of smoke, and the smells of roasting chicken and fish. After Judgement Day there wouldn't be any need to feed yourself . . . why not use up what you had? Others who weren't so sure about what God was up to had kept their stores intact, just in case.

Brother Gregory disapproved both of feasting and of hoarding things up.

'Oh ye of little faith . . . what need have you to hoard up treasure on this earth? Especially today?' he grumbled.

The whole festival atmosphere tasted of disrespect to him. But he was looking forward to seeing the punishments later on.

The Blessed Judith was in a state and, despite having already confessed three times that week, insisted on rushing out and getting done again just as they were ready to go. By the time they arrived the hillside was already crowded, but Edwin had saved them a good place. There was a wooden bench to sit on, the cross was only about twenty feet behind them and, best of all, they had a good view of the Abbot's bonfire.

They settled down in the warmth to wait for the world to end.

The sun went down. Fires blossomed brightly around the hillside. Tom wandered around with wide eyes, soaking up everything. Everyone was preparing in their own way. Some were praying, or singing hymns or chanting. Brother Gregory was rushing about preaching hellfire and scaring people silly. A group of children asked Tom to take them to the Abbot to ask if it was all right to cheer when God came into view, but the Abbot thought not.

'Cheer in your minds . . . a sort of prayer cheer. He'll hear it,' he said.

'It's not the same,' grumbled one of the children. But the Abbot always had the last word.

The night wore on. Tom got tired and curled up to watch landscapes inside the bonfire ashes. Midnight was the expected time for the world to end. As the hour approached, everyone fell very still. A group of vigilant monks led by Brother Gregory went around kicking out people's fires, on the grounds that they would dim the Heavenly Lights, but they didn't dare put out the fire that kept the Abbot warm.

Midnight came and went and there was no God . . . only loud complaints that the monks had left everyone cold.

The fires sprang up again and the long night wore on. It got cold and a handful of villagers started to pack up and go home, to the fury of Brother Gregory. But once the first few had gone, more followed. By the small hours the crowd was getting thin and Gregory was having hysterics. The last thing he wanted was the monastery let down on Judgement Day by a small crowd.

Then, at last, a thin skein of light appeared in the east . . . but it wasn't the end at all, it was sunrise. The night was over, the day had begun. The millennium had passed and no Second Coming. Life continued after all. A low moan of disappointment went up over half the crowd, a murmur of pleasure over the other. The Blessed Judith had perked up no end and was being tickled by Edwin. Like a lot of folk, she hadn't been keen on being judged. As the light brightened, the mood of relief grew and people began to joke and laugh. The Abbot, who had been disappointed to start with, was roaring with laughter at a joke someone told him. Then he stood up, shook out his cassock and lifted his arms to sign that he was going to speak. The crowd quietened. But before the words left his lips . . .

'Look! There! Here they come. The angels!'

Brother Gregory had risen to his feet and was pointing fiercely across the water. There on the horizon the clouds seemed to part and a host of slow white wings, caught in the silver and rose rays of the new day, were coming down from heaven. A low moan of fear spread among the crowd.

'Oh, ye of little faith! Prepare to meet thy maker!' screamed Gregory.

It was true. The angels were unmistakable. They were about fifty or sixty strong below a dappled ceiling of rose-edged clouds. As yet some way off, they passed through sunbeams of gold and rose and pearly white and seemed to magic-ally change in size and appearance as they approached. Their slow wings carried them forward at speed.

The crowd fell to their knees. Tom was staring

in amazement. It was true, it was true, it was true after all!

'Bow your heads to God!' bellowed Gregory.

But there wasn't a soul there who could resist a peek.

The angels were flying straight towards the cross on the hill top, their wings beating steadily. They were flying in a V–formation, their white feathers shining in the light, their long necks straining forward as they rushed over the rosy ocean.

Their long necks?

'Hang on a minute!'

Someone jumped to his feet. Every head lifted.

'. . . They're not angels. They're swans!'

Yes, yes, swans! They were swans after all. A great flock of them flying low out of the cloud, as beautiful and serene as angels, but no angels themselves. Someone laughed. Then another.

'Swans, swans, you old fool!' whispered Edwin to Gregory.

But there was still a thrill of fear on the hillside. The swans were so beautiful and so wonderful. Perhaps they were the real angels after all . . .

Perhaps they would turn into angels as they flew by. Anything was possible!

Everyone fell quiet again as the swans grew closer, bigger, nearer. They swept so low that you could hear the wind whistle in their pinions as they passed overhead. Then suddenly they were past, the sun on their backs. They were flying inland to feed.

The hillside was silent. The dawn, the silver light, the magical appearance of the swans had made everyone feel the same thing . . . that God had come to bless the world, not to judge it. The birds were His prayer to them. There was a long, still moment, as every head turned to watch the swans go about their business.

Then there was a murmur and the laughter began again. 'Pretty angels, Brother!' someone shouted to Gregory, who had gone as white as a sheet.

'Damn!' shouted Gregory suddenly. 'Damn! Damn! Damn!' He had been looking forward to this all his life . . . and now it hadn't happened.

All across the hillside, people were packing up. The Abbot got on with his speech.

'Well,' he said, smiling. 'It looks as if God didn't find us fit for the judging this time. Go home, go home, and enjoy yourselves.' He smiled at Brother Gregory, who was staring intently into the east, in the hope that the angels were still on their way. 'I'm afraid, Brother Greg, that you'll have to wait another thousand years.'

'Better luck next time, Brother!' shouted someone.

Gregory was furious . . . with the Abbot, with the crowd and with God Himself. He'd never felt so let down in his life.

But Tom was entranced. The swans had been like a miracle, flying out of the low clouds and sea mists and on overhead. He was sure they hadn't come just by accident.

'What do you think? What do you think?' he asked Edwin. 'Did God send them?'

'Who knows? Sometimes I think maybe God's a bit of a tease Himself,' said Edwin with a wink. He walked across to comfort Brother Gregory, who had hoped to see God and had been shown just a flock of swans instead.

Katherine Paterson

THE GIANT AT GOJO BRIDGE

Kyoto, Japan, 1174

I chose to write about the meeting of Benkei and Yoshitsune because I think it's a story that few people in the West have ever heard. There are many stories about Benkei and Yoshitsune, which date back to the twelfth century, the time of the wars between the Heike (or Taira) and Genji (or Minamoto) clans, and they are among the most often told and best-loved stories in Japan. You will find them retold in every art form – drama, music, art, poetry and prose. It is significant that the modern Japanese flag combines the red banner of the Heike and the white of the Genji as a red sun in a white field.

The scene is a bridge, lit only by the moon. The place is Kyoto, the ancient capital of

Japan. The year is 1174, or near about that time. Two figures are seen. One is enormous, perhaps eight feet tall. He is clad in the armour of a warrior, to which a long halberd is bound. He carries several long swords. The other figure is slight. Can it be a girl? It is hard to tell in the moonlight, but perhaps it is one of Kyoto's famous dancing girls, judging from the robes, and surely the long implement in its hand is a flute. But the gigantic warrior doesn't seem to think the other is a mere dancing girl. He is thundering out a challenge.

'Who dares to cross the Gojo Bridge at night?'

The voice that replies is that of the flute.

The warrior is enraged. 'If you value your life, turn around and go back to where you came from.'

The flute sings out merrily once again. The musician does not move.

'Do you see these swords?' the giant cries out. 'They are only a few of the 999 swords I have won from fools who have dared to cross this bridge. I will not tell you what happened to the men who once carried them. Begone, I say. I do not like to kill children, but I am not a man of patience, and you are sorely trying what little I have!'

Once more the only answer is a cheerful tune.

With a roar, the warrior lunges towards the defiant youth.

Wait! We cannot go on with this scene until you know who these two are, there on Gojo Bridge in the moonlight.

The giant is called Benkei and he is both famous and infamous – famous for his size and strength, and infamous for his ferocity and cruelty. Some say that his father was a *tengu*, those fearsome creatures with great long noses who are part bird and part man. They live among the evergreens in the mountains of Japan and may be either friend or foe of humankind according to whatever whim takes them. Those who believe that Benkei is the son of a *tengu* will also say that he spent thirteen months in his mother's womb and was born with a full set of teeth and black hair falling to his shoulders. At any rate, we know that as a baby he was so much trouble that he was given the nickname Oniwaka, which means 'Young Demon'.

Indeed, he was such a wicked child that when he was about nine, he was taken to a tiny mountain island and there abandoned. On this island pine trees grew thickly, crowding out the sun – just the sort of place that *tengu* delight in. But the boy Benkei was not frightened. Indeed, he played fox and geese with the *tengu* who lived there, and they in turn taught him many tricks which he used later in battle.

But the day came when Benkei wished to return to the mainland, for he remembered a loving mother who cared for him no matter how badly he behaved. It was easy for him to escape, for when he was brought to the island he had hidden many stones in his kimono sleeves and skirt. These he now dropped into the sea, forming a bridge back to shore. To this day the island with its narrow land bridge remains. It is called Benkeijima, or 'Benkei's Island'.

Benkei continued to grow. Some say he is now eight feet tall, others ten. Whichever is true, he is taller than any other man and so strong that he has driven iron nails into stone with his fist. He never flees from any foe, but in pursuit he can outrun the wind itself.

When he was young, the only human tenderness he knew was from his mother, but she died when he was seventeen. Benkei built a shrine for her and declared her a goddess, but he could no longer bear to live in that place and so went into the wider world to seek his fortune.

It might seem surprising that a boy known as Young Demon should grow up to be a monk, but Benkei is not an ordinary priest. He belongs to a group of warrior monks who live on Mount Hiei and spend much more time fighting and raiding other monasteries than saying their prayers. A previous emperor once said that there were three things he could not control: the waters of the great Kamo River, dice and warrior monks.

Like many of his fellow warrior monks, Benkei loves nothing more than a fight, and as large and as strong as he is, he has never lost a duel. In search of more conquests, he has come down into the city of Kyoto. Every evening he stands on Gojo Bridge, daring other warriors to try to cross. If Benkei wins, as he always does, he confiscates his opponent's sword. At the latest count, he has collected 999 swords. And if that young flute player has one under his cloak, Benkei will soon have an even 1,000.

But who is the mysterious flute player who dares to challenge the giant at Gojo Bridge this moonlit night? In 1160 Kiyomori, the great chief of the Heike clan, defeated Yoshitomo, the chief of the Genji clan. Yoshitomo's two elder sons also died in the conflict, but Kiyomori took pity on Yoshitomo's widow and allowed her and the three younger boys to live, though the children were taken from their mother and separated from one another lest they grow up to plot revenge against the Heike.

The youngest, called Ushiwaka, was still a baby when his father died. He grew up serving the monks in a mountain monastery far from his mother, far from anyone connected to the Genji clan. It was Kiyomori's intention, of course, that the three surviving sons of Yoshitomo become monks in peaceful monasteries far from the capital. But somehow, even as a little boy, Ushiwaka knew that he was destined to be a warrior. He made himself a wooden sword and crept out into the forest to practise.

The old *tengu* of that place watched the child practising with his toy sword. At last he approached the boy and asked him who he was and what he was doing. Ushiwaka showed no fear at the sight of a dreadful *tengu*. 'I am the son of Yoshitomo of the Genji,' he said, 'and someday I shall be a warrior and avenge my father's death.'

Now for some reason, this particular *tengu* had always preferred the Genji to the Heike, who were now the rulers of Japan. Moreover, he was impressed by the child's bravery and determination, so he instructed his own *tengu* warriors to teach Ushiwaka not only how to fight but all the secrets of warfare that only the *tengu* know. So from that time on, Ushiwaka would steal into the woods and learn from the *tengu* all the martial arts befitting a warrior.

He was a small boy and is now so slender a youth that he is easily taken for a girl. So recently he disguised himself in girls' clothing and ran away from the monastery. He has come to Kyoto, looking for his brothers and those remnants of the Genji clan who have remained loyal to his father's memory.

He had not been in Kyoto for many days before he heard of the giant at Gojo Bridge. All Kyoto is talking of Benkei and his latest conquests, and the brave boy, or perhaps we should call him the rash boy, could not resist trying his arts against the largest, strongest warrior anyone had ever known. And so now we find him playing his flute on Gojo Bridge, taunting the mighty Benkei.

I shall make a game of it, Ushiwaka thinks, as the giant lunges towards him. He thrusts his flute into his sash and, dancing to one side, he kicks out, loosening the fastener that holds Benkei's halberd to his armour. The spear-like weapon clatters to the wooden beams of the bridge.

The angry warrior drops his swords and retrieves the halberd. 'So, puppy, you want to feel the strength of my arm?' he cries. He is almost upon the youth, the point of his halberd aimed at the boy's heart.

Calmly Ushiwaka reaches inside his cloak, pulls his short sword from its scabbard and, leaping forward, parries the thrust of the halberd. Again, Benkei charges, and again, Ushiwaka counters his blow. Each time the giant is sure he will score, the boy manages to knock aside the blow with his small sword.

The exhausted warrior steps back to gather himself together. This time, I will surely get the little wretch, he says to himself, rushing at the boy with a mighty roar: '*ARAAAAAII!*'

But Ushiwaka steps nimbly aside and the point of the halberd is caught in his skirts. Benkei pulls it out and slashes away. The skirts are in tatters but the boy is quite unharmed, now leaping into the air, now dancing aside, now rolling on the bridge out of reach of the dreadful weapon.

At last the halberd simply falls from Benkei's exhausted grasp. He can fight no more.

'Who are you?' he asks the youth, panting. He prostrates his enormous body before the victor. 'I have faced the mightiest swords in the land and you have defeated me with a blade hardly longer than the stinger of a bee. Who are you who looks like a girl and fights like a *tengu*?'

The youth laughs heartily. 'I am Ushiwaka, youngest son of Yoshitomo of the Genji. My flute is longer than my sword and both, as you can see, are far longer than my nose. I am not a *tengu*, but, like you, I owe much of my knowledge of warrior arts to *tengu* teachers. Now, pick up your weapons and let us be friends instead of enemies.'

But the giant stays prone, hardly lifting his face from the boards of the bridge. 'I humble myself before you, sir. From this day I leave Mount Hiei and the company of warrior monks and become your slave for all the lifetimes that Buddha shall prescribe for me.'

Benkei more than kept that promise. In the years to follow, the boy Ushiwaka grew up to become Yoshitsune, the mightiest of all the mighty warriors of the Genji clan. Yoshitsune, with Benkei always at his side, joined forces with his older brother, Yoritomo, to avenge their father's death and bring Japan under the banner of the Genji clan. Benkei and Yoshitsune were famous for their cunning strategy as well as their bravery, but they will always be best remembered for their friendship.

Once victory was secured and Yoritomo became the first shogun of Japan, you would have thought that he would heap rewards on the two great warriors who had brought this triumph to pass. Instead, Yoritomo became insanely jealous. He sent an army to hunt them down and kill them.

Yoshitsune and Benkei fought long and valiantly, but what are two against a multitude? In the end, the giant and the flute player who had met so long ago at Gojo Bridge died, as they had lived since that night, side by side.

Since there are many versions of the story of Benkei and Ushiwaka at the bridge, I've gathered together as many sources as I could lay my hands on and made a patchwork. Some of these sources include Japanese Mythology *by Juliet Piggott (London: Paul Hamlyn, 1969),* The No Plays of Japan *by Arthur Waley (New York: Grove Press, no date given),* Folk Legends of Japan *by Richard M. Dorson (Rutland, VT: 1962),* Japanalia *by Lewis Bush (Tokyo: 1959) and a story I read many years ago in Japanese that I can no longer locate which included the detail that Ushiwaka was dressed as a dancing girl and carried a flute.*

Nigel Hinton

DARK HEART

England, middle of the fourteenth century

The Black Death. Even the name is frightening. I first heard about the disease during a history lesson. The teacher told us that it had wiped out a third of Europe. 'That means ten of the thirty people in this classroom would have died,' he said. I've never forgotten that chilling moment. Ordinary life can be filled with problems, but some people have had to cope with things more terrible than, hopefully, we'll ever know.

When I was nine I did a terrible thing. People call me a seer. And it is true, I know things.

I know when the weather is going to change. I can touch a ewe and know if she will bear healthy lambs. I know where water is buried in the earth. I can lay my hands on people and know what ails them and which plant will make them well. Sometimes I can heal them by touching them.

It is a gift. It is a curse.

I had it from my mother, who can do the same. And she had it from her mother. Who had it from her mother. Who had it from her mother. All the way back to the time before time.

And people marvel at this gift and fear it. And they call me Abigail the Seer. And they marvel at me and fear me. And I want to tell them it is nothing. For it *is* nothing.

I am a seer but I did not see what I should have seen when I was nine.

I did not see it because it was hidden in the darkest place on earth – inside the human heart.

For the first eight years of my life I travelled the countryside with my mother and father. We had a wagon and a horse and we made a living wherever and however we could. Sometimes if there were fairs or markets my father would juggle and do tricks, or he would play the pipe while my mother sang and I danced and collected the coins that people threw. But there were never many coins, because the people who stopped to watch us were as poor as we were.

My father loved performing, but most of the time he had to turn his hand to other work. Oh, he could do anything, my father, and he had a ready smile that opened hearts and made people want to hire him. And he was a willing worker who could mend broken furniture or help build a house or plough fields or harvest crops.

It was a hard life and there were times when we went hungry. In some villages there was no work and in others the villagers did not take kindly to strangers and drove us away. And on the road we lived in danger of being set on by thieves, even though we had precious little to steal.

But my father loved the life. 'I come and I go like the birds,' he said. 'I am no serf. I am free.'

It was winter when my brother Tom was born – hard, cold winter, when our bones ached from the frost. Mother and Tom nearly died in the freezing wagon, but then warm spring sunshine beamed down and soft winds blew and they both recovered. But, for the first time, I heard my mother speak of leaving the road, of settling down in a village. My father laughed as if she were jesting and she smiled as if she might be.

But she wasn't jesting. As my eighth summer passed and the autumn nights grew chilly, my mother spoke again of her desire to stay in one place.

'But where?' my father asked. 'Where is as good as the open road?'

'Here,' said my mother, raising her eyes and looking round at the village where we had been helping with the harvest. 'Here is work a-plenty. The lord of the manor is building a fine new house and has need of strong labourers. And Abigail and I can find work at the farm, tending the animals or cleaning or cooking or . . . oh, there are a hundred things we can do, aren't there, Abigail?'

'A hundred ways of being a servant!' my father sneered. 'Why be a servant when we can be free?'

'Aye, free to starve,' my mother said sharply, and then softened the sharpness by smiling at him and taking his arm. 'Let us stay for the winter, just for the winter. Listen to Tom's cough – a hard winter on the road will kill him.'

I saw my father's shoulders sag, and my mother saw it too, for she slipped her arms round his waist now and looked up into his eyes, sensing victory.

'Abigail wishes it as well,' she said.

My father looked towards me.

He loved me, my father. I had feared he would love me less when Tom was born, for fathers love sons more – it is only natural. But his love for me had grown even stronger. He loved Tom, of course, and dandled him on his knee and kissed the top of his furry blond head and tickled him to make him laugh. But what he felt for me was special. Me, a mere girl child. I was the apple of his eye, as my mother was fond of telling me. I knew that if I wanted to stay, he would stay.

I looked at him and his eyes begged me to say that I wanted to keep travelling. But I looked at my mother and Tom and remembered how they had nearly died in the cruel cold of the wagon.

'Abigail?' my father asked.

'I want to stay,' I said.

My father took a deep breath and looked away across the fields to where the track snaked over the hills and into the forest. Then he turned back and smiled, a sad smile.

'We stay.'

We stayed. And my father got work building the manor house. The lord was pleased with his work and let us live in a small cottage. A cottage with clean, warm straw to sleep in. A cottage with thick mud walls to keep out the killing cold and to keep in the warmth of our fire. How my mother loved to sit near that fire with Tom on her knee and me by her side. She hummed tunes to us and stared at the red glow with a quiet smile on her lips.

And in front of that fire we had many visitors, for it soon became known that my mother and I had healing powers. All winter long we treated the aches and chills of the villagers, and when spring came we were in demand for our skills with animals. We never charged for our help, but people gave us little gifts when they could.

We were liked in the village and our happiness seemed complete.

Then one morning I heard my mother calling my name. I ran outside, frightened by the panic in her voice.

Our wagon had gone. My mother was on her knees, staring at the tracks that its wheels had left in the soft earth.

She opened her mouth but no words came out, just a long howl of misery.

I ran round the village, searching for him, but my father had gone. And gone with him was a woman of the lord's household. She was called Anne and, people were quick to tell me, she had been friendly with my father all winter. Anne, who was young and beautiful. So beautiful that the lady of the manor had been moved to give her some of her own dresses. Anne, who had dazzled my father in those dresses. Anne, who had won his heart. Everyone had known it except my mother and I.

We, who were seers, had seen nothing.

I knew that my mother slept little and wept much, for I heard her at night as we lay together in our bed of straw. But, at the age of nine, I was too caught up with my own pain to care about hers. My heart ached for my father — for his flashing smile, and the rumble of his laugh, and the warmth of his strong arms, and the tenderness of his hand as he stroked my hair.

Mother, Father, Tom and I — we had been a whole. We had been secure, complete. And now the security was gone, the completeness was broken. I felt lost and scared by the world.

Week after week my heart ached. Week after week I asked myself what I could have done wrong that he would leave me. Week after week I tried to hide the tears that kept brimming in my eyes.

Then came the day of my shame.

I was alone — my mother and Tom were at the manor, where she had gone to beg the lord to let us stay in the cottage. I heard hoof beats, then a knock on the door. I ran to open it, my heart fluttering with hope that it was my father.

It was Anne.

She was holding the reins of our horse but there was no sign of the wagon. No sign of my father.

I made to close the door, but she put her foot against it and began talking fast.

There was little time to waste, she said.

My father had sent for me.

He was waiting at an inn a few miles down the road where they had been staying all this time.

Tomorrow the three of us would set off for far distant places.

This way my mother could have the settled life she wanted and my father would have what he needed – the freedom of the open road.

It was my choice – stay here or go with them.

Anne looked anxiously towards the manor house and then back at me.

I stood there, torn in two. Torn between the joy of seeing my father and the pain of leaving my mother and Tom.

I could not make this terrible choice.

Then Anne said something else.

She told me that she had always longed for a daughter of her own. That if I went with them, she would treat me as a princess. That if I went with them, she would cut up her beautiful dresses and make me fine clothes of my own.

I chose to go with them.

I could tell myself that I went because I loved my father but I cannot lie to myself. I had not been able to choose between my mother and my father. What made a foolish nine-year-old girl choose to leave was the offer of fine clothes. That offer blinded me. I could not see into the darkness of Anne's heart, otherwise I would have seen the truth.

The truth that I was soon to discover.

She had not come because my father had asked her. She had come because she feared to lose him. He had stayed in that inn only a few miles away because he could go no further. He missed us too much.

He was on the point of leaving Anne and coming home to us. This was her last desperate attempt to keep him. She hoped that if my father had his beloved daughter with him, he could be persuaded to leave the rest of the family behind.

She was right.

When we arrived at the inn my father was slumped at a table. Anne called his name and he wearily lifted his head. Then he saw me and the sadness in his face turned to joy.

For a long, long time he held me and kissed me and begged forgiveness with tears in his eyes. And I cried and held on tightly to those strong arms.

Then Anne came and told us that the horse was hitched to the wagon and that we should start our journey while there was enough daylight. My father gazed at me and nodded, hardly hearing what she was saying.

And so we rode away.

My father went because I was there. And I? I was on that jolting wagon because I had been tempted by the idea of fine dresses. And every mile took me further from my mother and Tom.

We travelled far in the first months, driven on by Anne, who said she longed to see the sea. I think, in truth, she hoped to lure us aboard a ship to another country, where we could never think of going home. We reached the sea but we did not take a ship. Instead, we spent the next four years moving from port to port along the coast.

The sailors and traders were richer than country folk and they paid well to listen to my father play the pipe while the beautiful Anne danced and swirled in her fine dresses.

The dresses were important for the dance, Anne said, so they could not be cut up for me. But I did not want them now, for she had soon shown her true feelings towards me. She was jealous of the love my father had for me and she slowly poisoned it with hints and lies and complaints against me. His love never died, but Anne changed him and, as I grew into a young woman, he became distant.

How I longed for my mother then. And how I saw my young brother in every laughing boy I passed on the street.

Then, late one year, we heard the first rumours of a terrible disease that was raging across the seas. Sailors told us stories about foreign ports where people were dying in their thousands. They spoke of boils as big as apples, of skin covered in black spots, of people driven mad with the pain, of graveyards filled to overflowing so that the dead were flung into pits.

We shivered with horror, then crossed ourselves and thanked God that we were safe.

But we were not safe.

Just before Easter, in the year of Our Lord
1348, the Black Death crossed the sea and started
to fill our world with terror. The ports were the
first places to be hit, so we headed inland, running before the disease. But it seemed to fly with
the speed of the wind and it overtook us.

Anne was the first to sicken. I was not glad to
see her die, though many a time I had wished
her out of my life. But watching her writhe and
scream in agony for five days drove away all my
anger and left me filled with only pity and fear.

My father was numb with grief and I had to
force him to move on, thinking now to lead him
back to our village and home. We had not gone
more than four days when he fell to shivering
and became too weak to move.

His agony was brief. That evening he coughed
blood and by morning he was dead. I dug his
grave at the edge of a wood and buried him deep
so that no animal would disturb his body.

I prayed for his soul and begged God not to

send him to hell for dying without confessing his sins to a priest. Then I lay down in our wagon, waiting for my own end, which must surely follow.

But I did not die. One day of driving rain, the sun came out briefly. Its light struck the raindrops that hung in the trees. They glistened blue and red and yellow as if the trees were strung with jewels. And I knew I had been spared. I was alive and I had my life to live.

As the rain set in again I left the wagon and mounted our horse.

It was a long and terrible journey across a land of the dead and dying. A land of unploughed fields and wandering animals. A land of silence. A land where people fled in fear from each other. A winter land. But, finally, I arrived back home.

Our cottage was empty.

The lord, his lady and nearly half the villagers had died.

My mother and Tom were not among the dead. One of the women told me that a few days after I had disappeared my mother had packed our belongings and walked away from the village with my little brother. No one knew where they had gone.

I thought of setting out to look for them but I knew I would never find them. The world was too large and dangerous. Better to stay in our cottage and wait for them to come home.

On the day I entered the village, the Black Death claimed its last victim there. A few days later, two young people who had the disease began to recover. Spring flowers started to bloom in the meadow.

The villagers remembered my healing powers and they began to say that it was I who had saved the village.

I tried to tell them that I had done nothing, but they would not listen. And my little gift became a kind of curse to me. My neighbours are good to me and love me for my skills, but they think of me as magical. Different. They marvel at me and they fear me. I live among them, but I live alone.

They call me Abigail the Seer. Oh, how that name stabs my poor heart, for I remember what I did not see.

And I long for the one who could truly understand, the one who shares the curse-gift with me. My mother.

I know that one day she will come. I know this for certain, just as I know which one of the thousands of acorns on the forest floor will grow to be a mighty oak. One day I will raise my eyes and there she will be, coming down the road with Tom. They will see the flowers I have planted round our little cottage and they will know that they have come home at last.

This hope lives in my heart, like a seed lives in the earth waiting for spring to come.

I have lived through terrible times, but life is strong within me. Each dawn the world is new and fresh and beautiful, and I take hope.

For we must live in hope.

Berlie Doherty

GHOST GALLEON

East Anglia, now and 1588

One day I was talking to some children in their classroom in Goole and I saw a huge ship sailing across the fields. I asked the children to turn round and look as well, in case I was going mad, and they said it happens all the time. Later, their teacher told me that what I was actually seeing was a ship on the River Humber, which ran very close to the school. I couldn't get this ghostly ship out of my mind, however, and I started thinking about a time when a great deal of the farmland in the east of England, particularly lower down in East Anglia, had once been under water . . .

My home is on farmland, in the flat fens of East Anglia. They say that many years ago my fields were sea, and that tides rose and fell over the fields that sway with wheat and in the groves that are now tight with trees. I discovered this when I was twelve years old and staying for a time in this very house which now belongs to me, but which at that time belonged to my grandfather. It was in that same year that I discovered that my name, Charles Oliver, is not English but Spanish: Carlos Olivarez. But the story of how I came to have this name, and how I learned the truth of it, is almost beyond belief.

It happened soon after I came to the house. I had asked my grandfather if the Oliver family had always lived in that part of the country. Grandad didn't answer me at first; he seemed to be weighing the question up. And then he said, 'If you're asking that, then I think it's time I moved you up to the little bedroom at the front of the house . . . Just for a bit.' He had that way about him, that made him seem full of unfathomable secrets – people say I have that way with me too. Anyway, I didn't ask him anything more, and he didn't tell me, but that night my sleeping things were moved right up to the top floor of the house, into the little bedroom that my grandad said he had slept in when he was a boy. There was nothing special about this room. It was smaller than the one I was used to, and I didn't like it much. It smelt damp, and it was dark and dusty. I had the feeling that no one had slept in it for years – maybe not since Grandad was my age – sixty years back! The window looked out on to a grove of beech trees, and beyond that miles and miles of fields, and the long, dark horizon of the east.

It was because it faced east that I woke up so early the next morning, with the first streak of dawn pushing itself like needles into my eyes. It must have been about four o'clock. I couldn't get back to sleep again, and I lay in bed looking at the way the strange light cast reflections like ripples on my wall and ceiling. I remember thinking that it must be because of the angle of the light coming up through the moving branches of the trees. And the trees sounded different too, this side of the house. I could hear the wind sighing through them, and it was a comforting sort of sound to lie in bed and listen to, even at that unearthly hour.

★

It was a regular, gentle, rushing sound, with a to-and-fro heave to it; a rhythm. A kind of breathing, like the sea.

It *was* the sea!

I jumped out of bed and ran to the window. There was hardly any light to see by still, only that first pale streak where the sun would soon be, but the gleam of it stretched a sort of path over something that was dark and moving, rolling, slow and steady, and wave on wave of it, with here and there ghostly flecks of white. My sense told me that it was the wind moving across the fields of wheat, but my heart thudded in my throat with excitement and fear and told me that it was the sea! Yet the trees were there, black, between me and the skyline, and all I could make out was by peering through their silhouetted branches, and all I could hear of the waves was through the creaking of their tall trunks. And suddenly I realized that one of those trunks – no, two, three – three of the trunks were moving. They came gliding behind the pattern of the trees and were just visible over the tops, and as they passed behind a clearing my racing heart stopped, because what I could see now wasn't trees moving, with looped branches at all angles. Clear as anything, for that second when my heart stood still, I know I saw the masts and rigging of a sailing ship.

Even then I didn't realize how massive a ship it was till it came properly into view; then I could see that it had many decks, so the whole thing towered out of the water like a huge floating castle; and that it had three or four masts, each with its own cross-spars and sails. I saw it in silhouette, blacker than a shadow against the light, but so clear that all the tight ropes of its rigging traced a pattern like lace from spar to spar; like a cradle of fine web. And yet it was enormous. I'd seen pictures of ships like that. It was a ship of war of 400 years ago.

It was a galleon.

I raced down the stairs and out of the house with my pyjama jacket flapping open and all the dogs of the farm yapping after me. I ran till I came to the very edge of the grove, and fell back with weariness against one of the trunks, sliding my back down it till I was crouched on the ground. The sun was flooding up now, pushing up into the sky as if it owned the world, glaring out across not sea, but fields, as I'd always known, and the trees round me stood still and silent with not even a breath of wind to stir them. My thudding steps had sent rabbits scudding across the grass, white tails bobbing like flashes of light. When I could breathe steadily, I stood up again and looked across the flat plains. A harsh cry, like a sob, caught my attention, and I saw a great grey-white bird lift its heavy wings and drift slowly out across the line of the sun, and away out of sight.

'Heron!' I shouted after it in disappointment, and back came its strange, sad cry.

At breakfast I played safe.

'Grandad, I had a funny dream last night.'

'Did you, Charlie?' he said. 'What was it about?'

'I dreamt that the fields behind the trees were the sea.'

'Did you now?' said Grandad. 'Well, that wasn't such a funny dream. A long time ago, hundreds of years ago, most of this land *was* sea. All this farmland was reclaimed from the sea. If this house had been here then, the waves would have come lapping over the doorstep. And I should think whoever lived here would have been a fisherman instead of a farmer.'

I buttered my toast carefully. Had I known that already? I was sure I hadn't. But *had* I dreamt it?

I decided to pretend I wasn't much interested in the answer to my next question, in case it sounded silly.

'Would there have been galleons?' I asked carelessly.

'Oh yes. It's said, Charlie, that this coast was the route of the Spanish Armada, in 1588. They came right up here and over the top of Scotland.'

Long after my grandad had left the table I was still sitting there, still smoothing and smoothing a skin of butter over my cold toast, till Gran took it away from me and reminded me gently that there were farm jobs to be done, and that my help was needed.

So I kept my secret to myself. That night I

couldn't wait to get back up to my little room at the top of the house. I pushed up the window and leaned out. I could see the line of familiar trees, dark and quiet in the twilight. I pulled my chair over and sat there, my chin propped in my hands, staring out as the gloom gathered the sky into its darkness till there was nothing more to see, and nothing to hear in all that sleeping farmland.

I didn't know I'd gone to sleep till I was pulled awake by what seemed to be a cry coming out of the darkness. I leaned out of the window to listen again, but this time I caught that surge and sigh that I'd heard the night before – the wind in fields of wheat; or the waves of the sea, rolling. It was too dark even to see the trees. A gust of air brought in a cool dampness and, what's more, there was a tang to it, sharp and unmistakable with salt on its breath, and I knew what that was all right. It was the smell the wind brought with it when the tide was coming in.

And then, it seemed, I heard the cry again.

Again I raced down the stairs. I thudded down the track to where I knew the trees would be, even though there was no shape of them to go by. But light was beginning to come up, just a glow that was pale gold, and I knew then with a rush of fear that there *were* no trees, and that the cold sting on my cheeks was the fling of spray. I turned to look back and saw that the big old farmhouse building was gone, and that all that was left was the low shape of a cottage or hut, no bigger than one of our barns. But there wasn't time even to think about that. Water was lapping round my bare feet. I heard a massive creaking, and could just make out the shape of an enormous bulk moving somewhere far out in front of me, with little lights swinging on it, and the bark of voices coming from it, and into the line of the day's first light came gliding first the prow, then the hull, masts and all, and riggings, and straining sails, of a galleon.

For a moment the sun burst up. I saw the silk banners streaming scarlet and silver and gold, and the white sails arched back like wings in flight, and the lettering picked out in gold: *La Garza*. Spanish. Then a cloud dulled the sunlight and all I could make out were the poop lanterns gleaming like animal eyes, and the dark shape of it gliding quiet as death over the fields of my grandad's farm.

There was the cry again. This time I knew even before the light came up again what it was. A child was in the water and he was shouting for help.

I was a good swimmer, so my next action was completely instinctive. I never even stopped to think about the weirdness of the situation but waded out at once into the sea of 400 years ago, up to my knees, up to my thighs, and then I plunged myself in and swam out in the direction of the dark bobbing head.

'*¡Ay! ¡Socorro!*' the voice cried. I'd no idea then what the words meant, but they'll stay in my memory for the rest of my life. It's Spanish. 'Help!' it means.

'*¡Socorro!*'

There were times when I thought I'd never reach him. I kept losing sight of the bobbing head. Gulls' cries drowned his voice. The sea seemed to want to drag me down. But at last I did reach him, and he seemed to be half-dead by then. He had almost lost consciousness. I managed to hold him up somehow with my arm hooked under his armpit while I struggled to pull off my pyjama top. I'd been told at school how to make a kind of balloon out of it, but I never thought the day would come when I'd have to, or be able to. I kept going under with him, and the sea choked every breath I took. But at last I'd done it, and with both my arms round the boy I held on to the float and paddled for shore. I'd never swum so far before. I wanted to give up the battle and just leave go of him and let myself drift away and sleep. My body touched land at last, but I wasn't yet out of the sea. We were shored on a sandbank a few yards from the beach. Waves kept pulling me back and I hadn't the strength to pull myself any further.

And I couldn't have made those last few yards if a woman hadn't come running out of that little thatched cottage I'd seen earlier. She screamed something to me and waded in to the sea with her long skirts billowing round her. She caught us both by our armpits and dragged us out of the water and dumped us like big gasping fish on dry land. 'Mercy on us, lad, what's this ye've caught?' she said in the strange accent of long ago. 'Tha's fished up some sort o' monkey!'

I rolled over on to my back and lay gaping up at her till her shape swam into focus and I had the strength to pull myself into a sitting position. She knelt by the boy, marvelling at his olive skin, his black hair and lashes, his spoiled velvet clothes.

'He's Spanish!' I panted. 'Can you help him?'

'Help a Spaniard!' She spat into the sand. She folded her arms and rocked her head sideways as though she couldn't make me out either.

'Tha's asking me to help the enemy, son!'

I crawled over to the boy and lifted his head up. He coughed, and water streamed from his mouth like vomit.

'¡Ay!' he said weakly, lying back again.

'What a poor wretch he is!' The woman knelt by him and wrapped her shawl round his shivering body.

'You're all right!' I said to him. 'Don't worry. You'll be all right now.'

He opened his eyes at last. He looked terrified.

'You're in England!' I said. 'I'm Charlie. You?'

'Leave him be!' the woman said. 'He'll not understand thy talk!'

His eyes flitted from me to the woman and back again. He shook his head.

I pointed first to myself, then to him. 'Charles Oliver. You?'

'*¿Yo?* Carlos Olivarez. Charl Olibber.'

'Charles Oliver. Carlos Olivarez.'

'*Lo mismo.*'

'The same,' I said, and we stared as though we had always known each other.

The woman had moved away from us and was standing shielding her eyes against the early rising sun and looking out to sea. 'Methinks the boy will not return to Spain,' she said. 'See how his ship flies home!' Far away on the horizon now, right into the sunlight, the galleon scudded in full sail with all her banners streaming.

The boy Carlos pulled himself up with a terrible cry of grief.

'*¡La Garza! ¡La Garza!*'

I turned my eyes away at last from the retreating ship. The boy was gone, and the woman with him, and the little fishing cottage she'd come running down from. I was standing on grass, in our field, with our farmhouse behind us, and the field sloped down to a grove of beech trees, and beyond that field after field stretched out to the horizon, where the early sun blazed like gold and the great winged heron rose into its path with its sad and solitary cry.

In a daze I went back into the house. This time I knew I must tell Grandad everything. I waited downstairs for him, scared to go back to bed in case I fell asleep and came to think of all these strange things as a dream. But my pyjamas were wet, and my skin tasted salt, and I could still remember the weight of the drowning boy in my arms.

As soon as Grandad was awake I told him my story. He took it in his old quiet way, not surprised.

'Well, you've answered your question, Charlie,' he said. 'You asked me if our family had always lived here, and the answer is – yes. Since the time of the Spanish Armada. The first member of our family to live here was a Spaniard.'

'Carlos Olivarez,' I said.

'And now you know more than I ever knew,' Grandad went on. 'You know how he came here, and why he stayed.'

'He was a ship's boy off a Spanish galleon, and he fell overboard, and was rescued by an English boy and a fisherwoman.'

It was still too much to take in. I remembered the look on the woman's face, and the thought of how she'd pitied the enemy and taken him into her house. If she hadn't . . . if Carlos hadn't been rescued from the sea . . . he'd have died out there. And none of us would have been born. Not me, nor my dad, nor my grandad, nor any of the long line of boys stretching right back to the sixteenth century. The thought of it all made me dizzy.

'Grandad, did the same thing happen to you when you slept up in that room? Is that why you wanted me to sleep up there?'

He shook his head. 'I thought I heard the sea when I slept up there. It puzzled me, but I never saw it. Your dad heard it too, and as a child it frightened him. *My* father told me he saw the sea, and heard the creakings of an enormous ship of some sort. And we've all heard the same cry out there at dawn. I don't think anyone ever saw the ghost galleon before you did, Charlie. And I don't suppose anyone will now. It won't come back.'

'Why not?' I asked. In spite of all the terrible happenings of the night before, I felt that I wanted to see that beautiful ship again. I felt as if I belonged to it, and that the galleon belonged to me . . .

'Why should it?' Grandad said. 'The ghost boy has been rescued. No need now for the ghost galleon to come in search of him any more. Is there?'

I knew Grandad was right. 'I think I'll go down tomorrow morning, all the same,' I said. 'Just in case it's there.'

'You'll see something, but it won't be the galleon,' Grandad said. 'You'll see what I see every morning at dawn. I'll come with you, Charlie.'

★

Well, I did go down with him the next morning, and what I saw filled me with a strange sadness, as if I was remembering it from long ago. Till the end of my life the sight of it will fill me with the same grief. Grandad and I went down together to the grove and watched the startled white of the rabbits scurrying over the fields to safety. I saw the distant fields of wheat surging gold, like the sea with sunlight on it. I heard the wind sighing in the branches of the trees around me, like the breathing of waves. And when the sun was up I heard that strange, sad, half-human cry. I saw the heron lift its great heavy wings and drift out slowly towards the line of the sun, and what I saw then wasn't a bird any longer. It was Carlos Olivarez's galleon, *La Garza*: *The Heron*. It was arching back its sails like huge white wings and it was flying home on the winds of time to Spain. Without him.

Geraldine McCaughrean

THE LOST BIRTHDAY

In a village similar to many others all over England, 1752

Time is a man-made invention: we divided it up into hours, weeks, centuries. Arithmetically speaking, the new millennium won't begin on 1 January at all – not since Lord Chesterfield tore eleven leaves off the calendar in 1752. Hang on! Chesterfield moved New Year's Day from 1 March to 1 January too! So where does that put the 'True Millennium'? It all goes to show that momentous days, historic dates, aren't special in themselves – we just label them special. After all, who invented the word 'millennium'?

T homas was a clever boy, though not quite clever enough to understand why this made him unpopular. At school he was considered teacher's pet, because he learned everything the teacher taught and still thirsted for more. The teacher, Miss Trotter, might have liked him for this, if he had not kept asking questions she could not answer.

Old farmers who for decades had read the weather in seaweed and the colour of leaves did not seem to *want* to know what Thomas could tell them of cumulonimbus and barometric pressure.

When he stirred his mother's soup the wrong way – widdershins – saying, 'Only people can be superstitious, not the soup,' his mother slapped him.

Only his sister, Elizabeth, knew that Thomas was nothing but an ignorant boy. She was about to get married and naturally that meant she was too clever to bother with anyone, let alone Thomas.

So Thomas used to hang about near the seminary and the inn, and hold horses for lawyers and run errands for doctors, in exchange for information about the Magna Carta or bones. And whatever he learned, he shared only with

Gammer, his antique grandmother, who slept in a bed beside the fireplace. While he held her bowl, he fed her porridge and a diet of comets, biology, French and poetry. Since Gammer was seventy-nine and imminently expecting to die, she took in only the porridge.

It was Thomas who first heard tell of the alteration to the calendar. A traveller aboard the daily stage left his newspaper on a bench by the Red Lion, and Thomas took it home and read from it to Gammer – court engagements for the autumn of 1752, the war in Tibet, the invention of a lightning conductor . . .

'It says an act is going through Parliament to change the calendar, Gammer. To match the European one. By reason of the earth taking 365¼ days to go round the sun once, not 365.'

'What's that? What are you prating of, boy?'

'All those quarter-days have added up over the years. Seemingly the Pope made things right in Europe centuries back, but we kept to the old style. Now we are grown eleven days apart from Europe. And Lord Chesterfield wants to jump us forward eleven days.'

'Don't talk folly, child,' mumbled Gammer. 'A man cannot jump eleven days, no more than I can jump a five-bar gate. You have it all faddled in your brain.'

But sure enough, at church the following Sunday, Reverend Persimmon broke the same news to the village. 'An adjustment to the Julian calendar,' he intoned, 'bringing it in line with the Gregorian one.' Impatient to get on to his carefully crafted sermon, he did not trouble to expand.

As a result, no one listened to his sermon. A gradual crescendo of buzzing whispers swelled like a rising tide and washed away his oratory, until the Reverend Persimmon slammed shut his Bible and called for the last hymn as if calling for the Last Judgement.

'Cannot be true,' said the whispers.

'Take eleven days off us? He's mistaken, truly.'

'What man can do it?'

'Not the King himself.'

'Only God, sure. Never Parliament.'

'Not *eleven days*!'

'No, no. You don't comprehend,' whispered

Thomas. 'It is a way of reckoning things, simply. You see, the world takes 365¼ days . . .'

But they were not listening.

The farmers were aghast. 'How am I to finish harvest 'fore Harvest Festival, if you take me out eleven days?'

''Tain't true, or me marrows would be coming ready for picking.'

Mrs Baker clutched her mountainous stomach. 'What, the babe due any minute and the crib only half made?'

Thomas's mother howled and held her head. 'I feel it! I feel it! Eleven days nearer my grave!'

'Mam, you're no older than yesterday,' Thomas tried to explain. 'One day only. It's naught but a kind of arithmetic.'

'Oh, hold your tongue, noddle!' she snapped, clipping his ear. 'They rob us of our taxes and now they've robbed us of our days!'

Instead of walking directly home from church, the village foregathered in the yard of the Red Lion to exchange outrage.

'Oh, but, Mother!' cried Elizabeth, sailing against the tide of feeling. 'It's wonderful! Do you not see? My darling will be home any moment. And in three days, I shall be a married woman. I am going to watch for his ship!'

'He just set sail, Lizzie!' said Thomas. 'How can he get to Ireland and back in a day?'

But his sister only cast him a look of serene contempt and went to sit on a cliff top and await a ship not due back for a week.

Thomas ran to the rector's house. 'Come quick, Reverend Persimmon, and explain to them about the calendar! My ma and all are acting like the Three Sillies, and I can't make them understand. They think they've lost eleven days out of their lives!'

Mr Persimmon, a beaker of claret in one hand, sniffed loudly. 'Good. If they think they are brought nearer to Judgement Day, they may cast aside their sin the sooner,' he said, and shut the door in Thomas's face.

By the time Thomas got back, the whole village was in uproar. Even Miss Trotter was quacking like a duck. 'And if this be no longer Sunday, but Friday rather, why are the children not in school?'

Someone daubed a rude word on the rector's garden wall, and Dafyd Owen (who was a Baptist) called Persimmon 'a lackey of those despots at Westminster'.

'It is not Mr Persimmon's fault,' Thomas told his grandmother. 'They should not go blaming the rector for passing on the news.'

'News? What news?' asked the frail little creature, her strength too small to allow her a turn of the head. Thomas began to explain yet again, but the door of the cottage was flung open and his mother burst in.

'*We are to lose eleven days from our lives, Gammer!*' she wailed, hair all awry and her face tear-stained. 'And there's the wedding on top of us, and no time to do it, and the Sabbath's turned weekday, and those villains in London have delivered us whole days and days closer to the end of the world!'

'Gammer, take no notice. Ma doesn't . . .' said Thomas, but his mother came at him, swinging her bonnet by the ribbon.

'*Eleven days gone are eleven days gone!* Don't they bring rent day eleven days closer? And when you lie on your deathbed, my boy, you'll think it more than ill that those mongrels in London cut you off from the sweetness of light and breath eleven days too soon!'

'Eleven days?' Gammer sat up, her milky eyes brighter than they had been for a long time. 'What of my feast day? Am I not to be eighty?'

If her daughter had not worked herself into such a state of hysteria, she might have thought to say something soothing. But she was shrill with fright. 'Just so! Just so! No birthday for you, Ma! You must be seventy-nine still, and Lizzie must be wed without cake or bakemeats, and there shall be no fair-going for Thomas!'

'No fair?'

'Well, and how should there be a mop fair without the day where the mop fair should have been? Eh, noddle? Eh?'

All of a sudden, Thomas felt less cheerful about the change to the calendars.

The yard outside was filled with wailing, as though the Last Day might indeed have come sooner than expected, and Elizabeth came in weeping and moaning. 'Ship's lost! He's gone, I know it! Or he's left me and found another in Ireland! 'Tis the fourteenth, they're saying, and we was to be married day after tomorrow and where is he? Still gone? *Gone! Drowned, or deserted me! He'll never come back, I know it, and I shall live an old maid all my days!*'

'This house is like Bedlam,' said Thomas.

His mother and sister fell on each other's necks in an apoplexy of grief.

'Be quiet, you gooses.'

It was Gammer – and yet it was not Gammer. She had thrown off her blanket and was sitting on the edge of the bed, legs like dogwood, knees like crab-apples. 'Do I stand there yammering on, and leave the corbies to do as they please? Not while there's breath in me!'

'Gammer!'

She was pulling a scarf over her thinness of hair – fingers like spillikins, knuckles like five-stones – and a cloak over her shift. 'I set my mind to living eighty year on this earth, and will some Westminster rake have me wait on eleven months more before I see a feast day? Harlots and jackanapes! Nothing good ever came out of London, but this day's work we will push back down their throats! I'll take a broom to the King himself for stealing of my birthday!'

No spectre rising from its grave was ever so alarming as Gammer Coates the day she rose from her bed. Before anyone could restrain her, she was out in the lane, her piping voice exhorting the baker, the farrier, the sexton to 'Rise up and rout the government, you lummocks!'

What with his sister weeping and wailing, and his mother on her knees praying for hell to swallow up the rector, Thomas felt obliged to go after his grandmother, if only to be at hand when she fell down dead.

But he found her well down the road, walking at the head of a band of malcontents, fuelled by indignation and deaf to all reason.

'Where are you going, Gammer?' he panted.

'To murder the King!' said the farrier, who had been solacing himself with home-made gin.

'All by yourselves?'

'There will be more like us!' declared Gammer. 'No one will swallow such wickedness!'

'Come home, Gammer. Please!'

'Not till they give us back our eleven days!'

And before he knew what was happening, Thomas found himself swept along by their tidal wave of outrage.

In every town they came to, people who had been told the news (but not what to make of it) were reeling from the shock – people gnarled by old age or sickness, people who had already worked out the arithmetic of their lives and seen too many days gone from their allotted span to spare eleven more.

Thomas saw a side to his grandmother he had never seen before. All his life she had been the invalid beside the fire, silently, patiently awaiting her end. Now she was a firebrand, engaging total strangers in conversation, persuading them to revolution. The farrier and the baker turned back – they had trades to tend – but Gammer Coates trotted on, cheeks incandescent with zeal. And Thomas felt obliged to trot after her.

In Arrowby a doctor raised the shutters of his coach and asked about the commotion in the road:

'Give us back our eleven days!
Give us back our eleven days!'

He leaned through the window and shook his fist, calling Gammer 'a mad old witch' and 'a stupid, ignorant peasant'.

Thomas was so incensed that he began running alongside the coach, banging on the paintwork, bawling at the top of his voice, '*She is not mad! She lost her birthday, didn't she? Can you give it her again? Can you put off rent day either?*'

The doctor flushed purple, pulled down the blind again and shouted to the driver to put on speed. Thomas stumbled and fell behind. When he turned back, he was just in time to see Gammer Coates pick up a stone and throw it through the open window of the town hall. It landed in the mayor's soup.

Sitting in Arrowby lock-up, Thomas and Gammer Coates lost track of the hours. While they were there, Thomas had plenty of time to explain about the correction of the Julian calendar to bring it into line with the European Gregorian one.

But he did not try.

'The thing is,' he said, 'to take every heartbeat for a second. It's the only true, reliable clock.' Then, on the wall of the lock-up he multiplied sixty by sixty and again by twenty-four to show Gammer how many seconds she had lived each day of her life; how many years, how many heart-beats. 'And your heart has not ceased beating for eleven days, has it?' he argued. 'Therefore you must have lived to your eightieth by now.'

Gammer nodded reflectively, her smile huge as the calculations on the dank wall.

'But if we give 'em their way, they will have Christmas wrong ever after, boy – and New Year and fair days and the century's end . . .'

'It won't fret them,' said Thomas confidently. 'People are not fretted by what they don't know, only what they do.'

And Gammer nodded again and patted his hand.

When the circuit magistrate arrived, Thomas and Gammer were brought out of the lock-up blinking, to stand trial for riotous behaviour. When asked her age, Gammer did not hesitate.

'Eighty years today, Your Honour. We counted the heartbeats, we did.'

'Eighty!? Why, what is the constable thinking of, arresting a gentlewoman of eighty?' demanded the magistrate, frowning about the courtroom through his lorgnette.

The constable rose to his feet, flustered. 'I never thought she was above sixty, sir, honest!'

At which Gammer Coates beamed, radiant with happiness.

'I sentence you both to eleven days,' said the magistrate deliberately.

Thomas gulped. The lock-up was a very damp and unwholesome place for an old lady to pass one night, leave alone a week and a half.

'But in consideration of your feast day and your great age,' the magistrate continued, 'I stipulate that those days run twixt third September and its fourteenth in this year of our Lord 1752.'

He did not exactly wink, but the clerk of the court coughed, and the beadle snickered, and Gammer Coates beamed all the wider.

'My granddaughter's marrying in a heartbeat

or two,' she told the magistrate. 'If Your Honour is passing by Grovely way, we'd be right honoured if you'd set down your bum 'twixt me and the groom.'

'You are kind, madam,' said the magistrate with a gracious nod. 'You are more than kind.'

'That's if the lad is fool enough to come back from Ireland,' Gammer whispered to her grandson.

Josephine Feeney

JACQUELINE'S MOON

Leicester, England, July 1969

*As children we were fascinated by the Apollo space
programme – especially the race to land on the
moon. One clear, bright winter's evening, as I
walked home with my brother, Tom, we discussed
the current Apollo mission. Suddenly, Tom
stopped and pointed up at the sky. 'If you look
very clearly,' he said, 'you can probably see the
Apollo spaceship.' We stood and looked for ages
and ages.*

I think I saw it

In the summer of 1969 my best friend was
Jacqueline Richards. Jacqueline was a very
popular name in those days – there were five of
them in my class. They were all named after a
famous lady called Jacqueline Kennedy. But my

Jacqueline was the best. She was brilliant at double-ball, handstands, inventing new games and writing stories. She was a faithful friend.

I longed for the start of the big summer holidays in 1969 so that I could play out all day with my Jacqueline. My mum had other ideas. The first day of the long holidays, Mum said, 'Lydia, your fringe is getting in your eyes. Shall we go to Mr Carlyle?' I knew by the way that she'd said my name that this wasn't a question – it was an order.

I didn't want to go. 'I'm trying to grow it,' I said, peeping at Mum from one side of my fringe.

'It's a mess, Lydia,' Mum said.

'I know, but when it gets a bit longer I'll be able to tie it back . . .'

'If that's all you want to do you might as well get it cut.'

'I hate Mr Carlyle's . . .'

'Don't be difficult, Lydia.'

Mr Carlyle had his hairdressing shop in between the garage and Mrs Oxton's, the bakery. He talked and talked. He was always talking. He never even stopped to ask what style you wanted. He had only one style for girls and one for boys.

The hairdressing shop was like an ordinary house with a big window. Mr Carlyle had two big chairs in his front room, a small sink underneath a huge, round mirror. In one corner there was a pile of towels – he wrapped one round my neck. I stared at my reflection in the window.

'What's it to be today?' he asked brightly.

'Cut please, Mr Carlyle,' Mum replied. 'Nice and short. I don't want it in her eyes for the holidays,' she continued.

'Right,' Mr Carlyle said. When Mum settled on the other chair and started to flick through a magazine, Mr Carlyle asked, 'How's your friend Jacqueline, then?'

'She's very well, thank you.'

My mum was watching me as I spoke.

'It's a great time to be young,' Mr Carlyle stated.

I never knew what to say when grown-ups said things like that.

'Yes,' Mum agreed.

'When I was young,' Mr Carlyle began, 'there

were no houses past Claypit Road. It was all fields. Have I told you this before?'

He had. Every time I'd been for a haircut. In fact, me and Jacqueline sometimes pretended to be Mr Carlyle and we used to say, 'When I was young . . .'

'Yes, it was all fields, a grand place for playing out, but the youngsters didn't get much chance for playing in them days,' Mr Carlyle went on. 'No, we always had to be running errands. That's what I mean when I say, it's a great time to be young. How short do you want this fringe, Mrs Porter?'

'Nice and short, Mr Carlyle. We don't want it getting in her eyes during the holidays, do we, Lydia?' Mum said, smiling at Mr Carlyle.

'No,' I said, although it didn't matter what I said anyway.

'Take the moon, Mrs Porter,' Mr Carlyle continued. 'Youngsters have got all that to look forward to . . . I mean, they're setting off tonight, aren't they, from America and then they're going to land on the moon and walk on it. I was watching it last night –'

'Waste of money, if you ask me,' Mum said, hardly glancing up from her magazine.

'Oh no, oh no, Mrs Porter – you can't say that. I'll bet any money, by the year 1980 people will be going to the moon on holiday!' Mr Carlyle said. He was so excited with all this moon talk that he cut my fringe very badly. 'Oops, Lydia, just have to straighten it up a bit.'

Mr Carlyle cut my fringe really short. I knew Jacqueline would laugh as soon as she saw it. I felt very angry. I could hardly answer Mr Carlyle when he asked, 'Will you be watching, then, on the telly, Lydia?'

'I hate Mr Carlyle,' I said angrily, when me and Mum arrived back home.

'Lydia!' Mum said in her warning voice. 'Don't say you hate anyone.'

'Well, I do – look at the mess he's made of my hair,' I said.

'It'll grow, Lydia. He's a very experienced hairdresser, Mr Carlyle. He used to cut my hair when I was a girl,' Mum said. 'So if it was good enough for me . . .'

'You see, if he's that old, Mum, he shouldn't be cutting people's hair. He could be dangerous . . .'

'Don't be cheeky, Lydia,' Mum hissed. I didn't mean to be cheeky. 'You're not playing out with Jacqueline if you're going to be cheeky.'

'I don't want to play out with anyone. They'll laugh at my fringe,' I said quietly.

But when Jacqueline called for me, she didn't even notice my fringe. 'Guess what?' she said. She stared right at me. I couldn't think of anything to say. 'You'll never guess, I'll tell you. You know Terence Keane? His mum and dad have got a new telly and it's colour!'

'Colour?'

'Yeah – and guess what else? He said we can all go and watch it tonight, watch the children's programmes.'

'Tonight?'

'Yeah, well, about five o'clock, and Terence's mum said we can bring our mums and dads too, if they want to come.'

My mum didn't want to go. She said, 'You

can't make the news any better just because it's colour.'

Everyone, apart from my mum, was there. Even Mr Carlyle was in Terence's front room.

'I'll be interested to see what the moon looks like in colour,' Mr Carlyle said.

'He's mad on the moon,' I whispered to Jacqueline. 'He kept on about it today when . . .'

'I thought your face looked a bit funny,' Jacqueline said. 'It's your hair, isn't it? Still, at least you've got six weeks for your fringe to grow.' She was kind, my Jacqueline.

'Jacqueline, I'm sure you don't talk like this when you're at the pictures,' Mrs Keane said. 'If you did you'd get thrown out.'

'Sorry, Mrs Keane,' Jacqueline said.

It was like being at the pictures, sitting in Terence's front room, staring at a colour television, even if it was all about the moon. It wasn't a real colour television, the sort we have now. No, it had a sort of plastic colour screen over the front of the television to make the black and white pictures more colourful. Mr Keane had brought it back from his aunt in Ireland.

'If you like,' Mr Keane said without moving his eyes from the television, 'you can all come and watch when they land on the moon.'

'That's very kind of you,' Mr Carlyle said. 'I'll look forward to that.'

'We could make some sandwiches and have a bit of a party,' Mrs Keane said.

'Good idea,' Mr Keane said. 'Let's have a party!'

For the next few days, everyone on the street was talking about the moon and the Keanes' new television. Jacqueline and I played double-ball against the Painters' huge, iron garage door.

'Are you going to the telly party, Lid?'

'Are you, Jack?'

We always called one another shortened names when we played double-ball. Otherwise it was too hard to concentrate.

'No. Mum wants to go, so I'll have to stay and look after the little 'uns,' Jacqueline said.

'I'm not going if you're not going, Jack.'

Then Mr Painter started to wind up his garage door.

'Will you girls go and play down your own

end!' he shouted. 'You're giving me a headache.'

Jacqueline and I stood and stared at Mr Painter.

'Well, go on, then. Clear off down your own end!' he shouted.

We walked slowly away. I had thought about answering him back, but I knew he'd march me home if I did that. I looked back to see him watching as we turned the corner into Jacqueline's entry. There was nowhere else as good as Mr Painter's garage for playing double-ball.

Jacqueline stared down at her tennis ball. 'Why is everybody watching it on the telly?'

'Watching what?'

'The moon.'

'I don't know,' I said, shrugging my shoulders.

'I mean, it's only up there, isn't it?' Jacqueline pointed up towards the sky.

'Yes.'

'Well, why don't we watch it ourselves?'

'Do you mean on your telly?' I asked.

'No! We've got a brilliant view of the moon from our attic. I watch it all the time. I can see all the mountains and lakes . . .'

'Have you got a telescope, then?'

'No, I use my dad's binoculars, but you're nearer to the moon when you're in the attic,' Jackie replied enthusiastically. 'I'll go and ask Mum if you can come and stay with us.'

'What about my mum?' I shouted after Jacqueline, but she didn't hear me – she was running across her back yard and into the back door.

'Mam! Mam!' she shouted.

I followed her, knocked on the back door and, when nobody answered, walked quietly into the kitchen. Jacqueline's dad sat at the kitchen table, reading the paper.

'How are you, Lydia?' Jacqueline's dad asked.

'Fine thanks, Mr Richards,' I said. He looked back at his paper. 'Jack's come to see about the moon, watching the moon,' I said, by way of explanation.

'I hear the Keanes have a new television. Have you seen it yet?' Mr Richards asked.

Before I had a chance to answer, Jacqueline ran into the room. 'You can! If your mum says it's all right, you can stay here for the night and we can watch the moon!'

★

On 20 July 1969, Neil Armstrong and Edwin Aldrin Jnr became the first men to walk on the moon. Me and Jacqueline watched from the attic bedroom of 23 Swan Street. We took it in turns to look through the binoculars. While the rest of the world watched it on television, or on cinema screens, me and Jacqueline sat on the attic bedroom windowsill, with heavy black binoculars glued to our eyes.

When it was Jacqueline's turn with the binoculars, I looked down at the front room of Terence's house. Shadows seemed to jump out of the house and people stood on the doorstep, desperate for a view of the amazing happenings.

'Can you see anything?' I asked Jacqueline for the hundredth time.

'Don't keep asking!' Jacqueline replied impatiently. She was a bit impatient at times, my Jacqueline. But we can't all be perfect, that's what my mum says.

'Where's the moon?' I said quietly. I didn't want to upset Jacqueline.

'I'm not sure – it might be round the back of

the earth, which means it'll probably show up in a few minutes.'

'And will we be able to see them then?' I asked hopefully.

'Oh yes,' Jacqueline said. 'They'll only look like matchstick men with a little blob for the buggy but we'll see them, don't worry.'

'It's very historic, isn't it, Jacqueline?'

'That's what Mr Carlyle says!' Jacqueline said, handing me the binoculars and laughing.

Just at that very moment, the clouds raced across the sky and the moon appeared. Jacqueline snatched the binoculars back. 'Told you, told you the moon was round the back of earth!'

'But it's my turn, Jacqueline,' I pleaded.

'Oh, all right, then, have a quick go,' she conceded.

After a moment, Jacqueline took the binoculars back and held them tightly to her face. For ages she didn't say anything, then suddenly, 'I can see them, Lydia! I can see them!'

'Who?' I asked, forgetting, for a moment, our true purpose in the attic.

'The moon men!' Jacqueline snapped.

'What do they look like?' I whispered.

'Matchstick men, but it's them . . . hang on a minute, I think they're shaking hands. Yes! They are, they're shaking hands!'

'Can I have a look?'

She reluctantly handed over the binoculars. I peered through them. I couldn't see a thing.

'Whereabouts are they, Jack? I can't see anything.'

She snatched the binoculars back again. 'You're not used to these, that's why you can't see through them. They're sort of in the middle, next to a kind of crater. If you'd got good eyesight and you knew how to use these binocs, then you'd be able to see them.' She stared into the glasses again. 'They're like matchstick men with big bubbles on their heads – that's their helmets. See if you can see them now, Lydia.'

'Oh yes . . .' I said quietly. 'In the middle. Are there two or three?'

'Two. You're not just saying that, are you, Lydia?'

'What?' I asked, surprised.

'You're not just *pretending* that you can see

them, are you?' Jacqueline asked, like a suspicious adult.

'No, I can see them – only it's hard if you're wearing spectacles too,' I said, handing the binoculars back.

'This is historic, Lid. Watching the men on the moon. I think they've gone into their car now,' Jacqueline said.

'I thought they had a rocket, Jack,' I said.

'Yes, but they took a car in the rocket – Dad told me. He read it in the paper today.'

'Must've been a big rocket! Where did they park it?' I asked.

'Round the corner,' Jacqueline said confidently. She had grown into a moon expert. 'The other man's in it. He's keeping it going while these two walk around . . . just in case they have to get away quickly. Do you want to have another look?' Jacqueline asked.

'No,' I said. 'I'd rather listen while you tell me what's happening.'

'OK,' Jacqueline said, settling into her space on the windowsill.

As she talked and talked about the men on the

moon, I realized where I'd heard that tone of voice before. When she had to look after her little 'uns and they asked for a story, that's just what she sounded like.

Jacqueline was brilliant at telling stories and that's why I was happy up there in her attic, watching Jacqueline's moon. It was much better than the real thing.

Beverley Naidoo

THE PLAYGROUND

South Africa, January 1995

When I was a child in South Africa, the whites-only government forced all children to go to segregated schools. White and black children were not meant to become friends. Over the years the prisons filled up with people, including thousands of black children, who fought to change the apartheid government. Many never lived to see what they had fought for. But in April 1994, for the first time ever, South Africans of all colours lined up together to vote. One of the most important laws the new government made was that all schools should be open to all children.

The word 'Dead!' struck Rosa as she drew near the cluster of children on the other side of the fence. She looked up and saw a boy pointing his forefinger at her through the criss-cross wire fence. He pulled his finger back sharply while his cheeks and lips exploded a short pistol blast. For a second she hesitated, her heart racing. She wanted to run. But that's what they were waiting for. Instead she forced herself to glance at all their faces. The narrow knife-grey eyes of Trigger-boy glinted with spite from under his corn-tassel fringe. But the others were more curious. Like cats hoping to play with a mouse.

Trigger-boy screwed up his mouth, preparing some new missile. Rosa pressed her lips tightly. She made herself walk steadily on, shifting her gaze into the playground behind the fence. Why shouldn't she look inside if she chose? But with the children's laughter now breaking behind her, she felt hot and angry. And it was to this school that Mama wanted her to go!

The playground was alive with chasing, skipping, running, shouting. A few children sat quietly on benches in the shade of lacy jacarandas that formed a boundary of pale green giant umbrellas between the tarmac and the playing fields. The well-kept grass stretched from the main road as far as a line of distant bluegums. They were the same tall grey trees that Rosa saw as she crossed the rough dry veld separating the township where she and Mama lived from what she had always known as the white people's town.

It was lunch-break at Oranje Primary School. Inside the grand double-storey, orange-tinted brick building with its neat rows of sparkling windows, children had classes both morning and afternoon. Not like in her school. *Her* school had so many pupils they had to take turns to use the classrooms! When she and her classmates finished lessons at twelve, the afternoon children were just arriving. There was no playground to talk of, just a stretch of dry ground and a few straggly cactus plants in front of a long row of single-storey classrooms.

Rosa eyed a group of girls around a netball post, one poised on her toes and with upstretched arm taking aim. Normally she would have stopped or slowed down to watch. Or she would spend a little time looking out for Hennie. Usually she only had to check through the boys chasing after a ball. It was a little game that she still played, seeing if she could spot him. Of course, he never saw her. Or if he did, he never let on.

'*Dumela*, sis!'

The boy who sold newspapers to passing motorists at the corner lights called out to Rosa as she approached. His dark eyes, set deep in a pinched nut-brown face, seemed concerned. Had he seen? The road was quiet and he was standing next to his stack of papers in a faded blue T-shirt pitted with holes.

'*Dumela!*' Rosa greeted him before turning the corner.

She broke into a jog. She could no longer be seen by Trigger-boy's gang from here and she wanted to get away as quickly as possible. On her left, iron railings with slim black spearheads protected the stern archway entrance to Oranje Primary School. Even the yellow roses were forbidding, standing like soldiers in straight lines.

Rosa didn't want to be late. Hennie's mother might deduct something from the few rands she was paying her to look after the twins every afternoon. When Mrs van Niekerk had asked Mama a few months ago if Rosa could help, Rosa had been upset. She didn't want to go back there! But Mama had pointed out they would need every cent in the New Year. President Mandela's new law might say that all government schools would be free to every child, but Mama knew the people of Oranje.

'They'll tell us there's this fund and that fund. But we'll be ready. They're not going to keep their Oranje Primary School just for their Hennies. It's going to be for my Rosa too!'

Rosa had known Hennie since they were babies. At three they had played together. Mama used to take her every weekday to the van Niekerks. While Mama cooked, cleaned, washed and ironed, Rosa and Hennie had scampered around the garden, built castles in the sandpit, made houses in the dry donga at the end of the long garden. The van Niekerks had left that part of the garden as bush and by the time Rosa and Hennie were five, Mrs van Niekerk no longer worried if Hennie was out of her sight for an hour or two. They always came back as soon as they were hungry and Mama would pour them both milk and give them cakes or scones, whatever she had freshly baked. Hennie was now a big brother and Mrs van Niekerk was largely kept busy with her twin babies, Jacob and Paul.

Usually, Mr van Niekerk left home early, before Mama and Rosa arrived, and returned after they had left. Mama never took Rosa with her on Saturdays and Sundays. When Rosa was old enough to ask why, Mama had explained that Hennie's father 'liked quiet'. Rosa told Mama that she and Hennie could be very quiet. They could play all day in the donga. Mama had said that Hennie's father wouldn't like that. The few times Rosa had seen him, he had never smiled. Rosa decided she would not like to see him angry. Hennie had told her about his father's belt. How he had beaten him with it one evening after tripping over a rope the children had tied between two paw-paw trees to practise jumping.

'I didn't tell on you,' Hennie had told her, showing her the marks on the back of his legs with some pride. 'And Ma didn't tell him!'

'What would your daddy do to me?' Rosa had asked.

Hennie had answered by sharply sucking in his breath as he pulled back his lips to show his teeth. Rosa felt her skin tingle as they began to collect dry grass to make a roof for the new house they were making.

Their playing together came to a sudden end when one day Mr van Niekerk came home early. The two of them were dashing under the sprinkler, shrieking and pulling funny faces for the twins, who were sitting up in their pram and gurgling, when Hennie's father strode across the lawn. Like a thunderstorm, he swept Hennie up with one arm and began to smack him on the bottom with the flat of his other hand. Hennie's cries of laughter turned to cries of pain.

'*Wat makeer jy?* What do you think you're doing? Running around like a savage? Half naked with this piccanin?'

The words slapped Rosa too. Mrs van Niekerk and Mama had both come running from the house.

'Is this how you're letting him grow? It's time he learned to be a proper boy – and to know he's a *white* boy!'

Rosa saw Mama's shoulders rise ever so slightly. Mama had taken Rosa silently by the hand and led her away. Above Hennie's sobs and the babies' cries, she heard Mrs van Niekerk.

'They were just playing, Willem. Just children's games. Look how you've frightened them.'

After that, Mama left Rosa on weekdays with their neighbour, Mrs Moloi. She was a kind old lady who looked after a couple of younger children as well. Rosa liked them but missed her games with Hennie. It would not be long, said Mama, before Rosa would start school and have lots of friends of her own age to play with. But when the New Year came and Mama took Rosa, in the maroon school pinafore that had been her Christmas present, they were turned away. The headteacher explained there were already eighty six-year-olds in a room meant for forty. He took their names and said he was sorry but they would have to wait another year. So Rosa returned to Mrs Moloi. Mama let her wear her school uniform. She was growing quickly and it would be wasted otherwise.

Rosa asked Mama about Hennie.

'Is Hennie waiting to go to school, Mama?'

Mama did not answer at first but when Rosa asked again, she replied briefly, 'No. He started at Oranje Primary.'

Three weeks after Rosa returned to Mrs Moloi, a spirit of joy blossomed like an unexpected rainbow for a few days over the entire township. Neighbours and friends crowded into their tiny sitting room, while Rosa sat wedged on Mama's lap, watching a tall grey-haired man with a warm, serious but smiling face wave at them from the small television set. All around Rosa, people were crying and laughing. Unbelievable, they said. It was a day they had almost thought would never come. Nelson Mandela, the man the white government had locked up for life, was walking free from his prison! Here was their Madiba coming to help them. They prayed for him to chase away the heavy grey clouds thrown over their lives by the white people's government.

Four years later, when Rosa and Hennie were ten, for the first time in her life Mama stood in the same long winding queue as the van Niekerks and the white townfolk, waiting to cast her vote for their new government. A 'rainbow government', Mama told Rosa.

The nearer it got to the end of term, the more Rosa began to worry. Parents were beginning to change their minds about sending their children to Oranje Primary in the New Year. Thato's parents wanted to 'wait and see'. Maybe the new government would send extra teachers to their own school. Maybe there would be money to build new classrooms and buy books. There were rumours of trouble. Someone's father had overheard talk of a 'White School Defence Committee'. Nearly every white home in Oranje had at least one gun locked in a safe. Rosa herself had seen burly red-faced men in town with pistols strapped to their belts. Often they dressed from head to foot in khaki. With their wide-brimmed khaki hats, they appeared like characters from old war films. Mama had told her to keep well out of their way.

One night Rosa was rinsing the dishes under

the tap in the yard, when Mama called her.

'You can finish that later! Come and watch.'

Mama patted the cushion next to her on the small sofa. Rosa curled up close. On the television an interviewer was asking children what it was like to go to a school that used to be only for white children.

'At first I was scared,' said a boy with a stylish haircut. 'Ree-aally scared.'

He paused, biting his lower lip. The other children laughed nervously.

'I thought no one would be my friend. But now I have lots of friends,' he added with a broad smile.

'It was like that for me too,' said a girl with a serious bronze-coloured face and thick long black hair. 'You think no one will like you and they're probably thinking the same.'

'Indian children go to that school too, Mama.' Rosa nudged Mama.

'And *we* were wondering what *you* would be like!' giggled a girl with a mass of blonde curls. 'You know how people pass round stories.'

'Especially horror ones!' interrupted the stylish-haired boy.

'You see,' said Mama, during the advertisements. 'It won't be so bad, will it, Rosa?'

'But, Mama, those white children aren't like the ones at Oranje Primary.'

'My grandmother taught me an old Zulu saying: *"Umuntu ungumuntu ngabanye abantu"* . . . We are who we are in the way we treat others. Even here, people will begin to learn that too.'

The reporter was back, talking about schools that still took only white children. A boy with a missing front tooth stared cheekily at the camera.

'Soon your school won't be allowed to turn away black children, Andries. Do you look forward to making new friends?'

'There won't be any of them after eleven.' Andries grinned.

'Why is that?'

'It won't be nice for them at break.'

'What are you going to do?' the reporter asked calmly.

The boy's grin widened as he shrugged his shoulders. Rosa chewed her thumb.

'That's what they're like here,' she whispered under her breath.

Mama heard. She pulled her closer and hugged her. 'Not all of them, Rosa . . . and someone has to go first.'

At the start of the Christmas holidays, Mrs van Niekerk asked if Rosa would help take care of the twins all day, including Saturdays. As Mama had said, Mr van Niekerk hardly noticed her now she was just a *kleinmeid*. Even though she went home in the evening quite exhausted, she earned only a few rand more each week for all the extra hours.

'It must be nice for you to be with your mother all day and earn some pocket money!' Mrs van Niekerk smiled. 'I wish I could see as much of Hennie!'

Hennie, it seemed, spent most of his time playing rugby. Mama was forever scrubbing clothes covered in red dirt.

'He'll be our first Springbok in the family!' Mrs van Niekerk said proudly to some Saturday visitors.

Hennie looked a little embarrassed.

'That's if the blacks haven't taken all the places by then.' Mr van Niekerk spoke as if he was tasting a lemon.

Hennie glanced at his father but did not say anything.

Another time, Rosa overheard Mrs van Niekerk speaking to Mama in the kitchen about 'this silly trouble at the school'.

'It's good for the new government to make schools free. But I don't know why they must force children together in such a hurry!'

Mama's knife continued chopping at the same steady pace. Rosa marvelled at how she could cover up.

All through the holidays Rosa kept hoping that Thato's parents would let her start at Oranje Primary too. But one evening as they passed the paper-boy, Rosa read the headlines: WHITE PARENTS TO PROTEST. Mama stopped to buy a copy.

'Will your mother send you to school now it's free?' Mama asked the boy as she handed over her coins.

'My mother is dead,' he said gravely. 'If I go to school, I won't have money for food.'

A car hooted and he darted away to sell another paper.

Walking down their road for the first time in her new Oranje Primary uniform, Rosa felt everyone was staring at her and Mama. Old Mrs Moloi wiped her eyes and called out good luck over the wall. But a group of older boys, sitting on crates outside the supermarket, stopped chatting as they passed. She thought she heard one of them say 'whitey'. Mama took her hand.

'Don't let anyone take who you are away from you, my child,' she said gently but firmly.

As they crossed the veld and entered the town, Mama's hand gave Rosa small spurts of encouragement. Before they had even reached the corner of Oranje Primary, they could see a crowd of adults and children lined up by the front entrance. It seemed like Trigger-boy's gang had grown taller and bigger, a hundred times over. A small gathering of policemen stood a short distance away, next to a man and a woman wearing suits and each carrying a briefcase. The crowd by the gate were all white but some of the police were black, as well as the man in the dark suit. Everyone appeared to be waiting for something, including the paper-boy. He stood at the corner watching Rosa and Mama approach. He looked worried.

Mama squeezed her hand more tightly as they reached the protesters. Faces and placards became blurred, but Rosa couldn't blot out the hoarse screams: 'NEVER! WHITE AND BLACK DON'T MIX!' 'FIGHT FOR A WHITE ORANJE!' 'NO BLACKS HERE.'

Mama never turned her face. Rosa, however, took a quick peek behind her and saw that the man and lady with briefcases were following. At the top of the steps, under the entrance arch, stood a stern, grim man. His folded cheeks were shades of grey and his eyes, behind the thick glasses, reminded Rosa of a rhino standing guard. Was this the headteacher? She felt her stomach twist. A man with a deep red face under a large khaki hat was arguing with him from the bottom

163

of the steps. He jabbed his finger in Rosa's direction.

'If you let this one in, we'll take all our children away! I'm warning you!' He stretched out his arms to stop Rosa and Mama going up.

'If I don't let her in, the government will close the school! Don't you understand?' The head-teacher sounded almost like he was pleading. Then he glared towards the couple with brief-cases. 'We have no choice!' he said bitterly.

Rosa heard a clicking sound. A camera loomed towards her, clicking again.

'This has echoes of Little Rock!' A man with an American accent was speaking into a micro-phone. 'What's it like to come to a school where people don't want you?'

He thrust the microphone near her mouth.

'They will want me when they know me!' Rosa replied softly but clearly.

But before he could ask anything more, the man in the khaki hat started to push him violently away. The policemen rushed forward and the next thing Rosa knew was that she and Mama were somehow at the top of the steps, being hurried by the grim-faced headteacher into an office.

The forms filled in, Mama had to leave. She had to face the remaining protesters and then explain to Mrs van Niekerk why she was late. Rosa tried not to feel panic as she watched Mama go. She followed the headteacher in the opposite direction down the long corridor and up the stairs to the Standard Three classroom.

As soon as she entered the doorway, she saw him. Trigger-boy. He sat in the far corner of the room, gazing straight at her. Why couldn't he be one of the children whose parents took them away? Why did he have to be in her class? The teacher pointed to an empty place by the window two desks in front of Trigger-boy. Rosa saw everyone's eyes turn from her to the girl who would be sitting next to her. She struggled to remain calm as she walked across the room.

'Eyes on your work, class. I expect at least two pages by break.' The headteacher was still standing by the door. 'I expect no nonsense too! I want to hear no bad reports from Miss Brink.'

'Ja, Meneer Botha!' the class chorused.

Rosa heard a low snigger behind her as the headteacher left. Miss Brink looked young but severe. Her lips were a deeper red than her rust-coloured hair, which was pulled tightly back into a neat bun. Her heels clicked crisply against the floor as she walked down the aisle to Rosa with an exercise book.

'The title for your composition is on the board. Let's see how good your English is.'

Rosa stared at the two words: 'My Holidays'. She hadn't really had a holiday. Did she want to tell Miss Brink that she had been working as a *kleinmeid* at Hennie van Niekerk's? She was wondering whether she should make something up, when she heard Miss Brink talking to her.

'There's no time to sit around. I expect you to catch up with the others.'

The girl in the desk next to her caught Rosa's eyes and made a quick 'Better watch out!' face. It wasn't unfriendly. Carefully writing her name and 'Standard Three Oranje Primary School' on her new English book, Rosa remembered Mama's words: 'Don't let anyone take away from you who you are.'

Well, she would tell Miss Brink how she had spent her holidays. Although Hennie was in the class above, he would probably tell his friends and word would spread anyway. And it was nothing to be ashamed of. Rosa smoothed down the first page and began to write.

As soon as she started on the mischief the twins got up to, there was no stopping. Only once she paused briefly, peering out of the window past the lacy tops of the jacarandas and down to the playground. How strange to see it from this side of the fence! But she wasn't looking forward to going out there at all. If only Thato was with her. She returned to her writing. It took her mind off the coming break-time and when the bell rang, she had reached the end of her second page. Miss Brink asked if someone would like to take 'our new girl' out to play. The girl next to Rosa volunteered.

'Thank you, Marie,' said Miss Brink. 'And show her where to find the toilets.'

Rosa kept her eyes on Marie's mouse-coloured plaits as they tramped with the crowd down the stairs. Yet again Rosa was aware of people looking at her. They had just reached a corridor leading towards the playground, when someone tapped her on the shoulder.

'Meneer Botha wants to see you,' a girl panted. 'Don't worry, Marie. I'll take her.'

Rosa looked from the girl to Marie. Why was she being sent for? She was anxious but didn't want to show it.

'Come,' said the girl when Marie had left. 'We'll go to the office this way.'

The girl began to lead her along a corridor with Standard Four and Five classrooms. But it was after they turned into a narrow alley leading out into a deserted yard that Rosa became really worried. On one side was a windowless wall with a wooden door and two large metal bins. In the distance the playing fields stretched out, still and silent.

'But the office, isn't it near the entrance?' Rosa's pulse beat faster, as if sensing an invisible trap.

'Ja, it is. I'm just showing you round our school.'

The girl's voice was calm, except there was a

slight stress on the 'our'. Faint sounds of children's laughter and shouts came from the playground on the other side of the building.

They were half-way across the yard when Trigger-boy and a small posse of children stepped out in front of them from behind the bins. His elbows swaggered outwards, hands resting on hips.

'You!' he demanded. 'Come here!'

Rosa stood rooted to the spot, the knife-grey eyes burrowing into her. She was aware of the girl at her side shifting slightly, as if ready to grab her should she try to run back. Folding her arms, she clutched her sides. She hoped they couldn't tell that she was shaking inside as she stared back squarely.

'My name is Rosa.'

Trigger-boy wrinkled back his upper lip, showing his front teeth. Like a bulldog. 'What did you say?' he drawled.

She knew he had heard. Her lips sealed themselves and her mind raced desperately as five sets of eyes pinned her down. This time there was no fence between them.

'Anyone seen a rose this colour?' he sneered to the others.

'Yuk!'

'Do you think we can pick her?'

Trigger-boy snapped his fingers. His hand whirled like a crazy wasp. Rosa clenched her fists. She would fight them if she had to.

'Leave Rosa alone!'

She knew that voice! Swinging around, she saw Hennie stride out of the alley. His angry eyes and forehead were so like his father's! Even his voice had the same fierceness. Rosa's stomach did a somersault.

'Ag, Hennie, we're only playing,' whined the girl who had led Rosa out to the yard.

Hennie ignored her. Trigger-boy and his friends were suddenly deflated, like let-down balloons. Hennie turned to Rosa.

'The playground is that side. I'll show you.'

Before they were out of earshot, Rosa heard Trigger-boy complaining loudly. 'Just because he's in Standard Four and good at rugby, he thinks he can boss us around.'

Hennie took no notice.

'I saw you and your ma come to school this morning . . . with all those people.' He paused awkwardly. 'You were very brave.'

They turned the corner, following a path alongside the orange-brick building. Hennie walked a little more slowly. Rosa's heart was still thumping. She let Hennie's words sink in. They were coming to the playground and already Rosa could see children on the tarmac ahead glancing in their direction. She stopped and turned to Hennie.

'Somebody has to be first,' she said.

Before he could reply, there was a shout. 'Ag, Hennie, we're waiting for you! Hurry up, man!'

'I've got to go, OK?' Hennie's voice was low.

'Thanks, Hennie,' she said simply.

His face flushed a little, then he disappeared into a cluster of boys tumbling after a ball.

Rosa scanned the playground. She deliberately took no notice of the stares. Her eyes travelled across the tarmac, and beyond the children who were chasing, skipping, running and shouting, to the criss-cross wire fence. In the distance, she glimpsed the paper-boy slipping in between cars at the red light. On the way home she would ask him if something was in the paper. A broken placard rested lopsided against the wire. 'NEVER! WHITE AND BLACK ...' If the protesters came again, she would have to face them on her own. Mama couldn't keep on being late for Mrs van Niekerk.

But that was tomorrow. Rosa gave her head a little shake. One step at a time, as Mama would say. Her eyes reached the benches under the jac-arandas. A girl with mouse-coloured plaits seemed to be looking in her direction and smiling. It was Marie. Rosa took a deep breath. She stepped out on to the tarmac and crossed the playground.

Nina Bawden

THE ANGEL OF THE CENTRAL LINE

The Last Time I went on the London Underground in the Rush Hour

One bitter cold night this happened to me. I had to be in Notting Hill Gate. The taxi didn't come. I ran through the snow to the Angel tube station and caught a train on the Northern Line. I had to change to the Central Line at Bank but when I reached Bank station, the Central Line was closed. It was rush hour. And chaos. It was clear to me that the collapse of the cities was imminent. Then my angel found me . . .

This is a true story. I tell you this because I am afraid that otherwise you won't believe it. (I find it quite hard to believe myself, which is why I am writing it down so that later on in my life, when I am old, I will be able to read it and remind myself that it really happened.)

I had quarrelled with my best friend, Tom. It was the middle of winter. He lived in Notting Hill and I lived in Islington, but at that time, which was before the collapse of the cities, most outlying settlements were connected by the London Underground Railway, or, as we called it then, the tube.

I won't say what we quarrelled about because it has nothing to do with my story. All you need to know is that we had been sitting in a café close by Notting Hill Gate tube station when he said he never wanted to see me again in this life, and I said that I hoped I would never have to see him again in the next.

All the way home in the tube train I wished I was dead. As I opened the front door I heard the phone ringing and ran to answer it, but it stopped as I got there. 'Just as well,' my dad said, coming out of the kitchen. 'I told your mother we'd go to Tesco before she got back and we're running behind.'

I skidded round Tesco like an Olympic

sprinter, hurling bottles and cartons and cat food and Special Offers into Dad's trolley while he lumbered along at the speed of a very old man propped on a Zimmer frame. Dad groaned a bit, but he laughed as well, and when we got back he said he could see I had better things to do with my time than provision the household, so he would do his best to carry all the stuff in by himself.

There were three messages on the answer phone.

The first said, 'Just thought I'd ring.'

The second, 'You ought to be home by now. Oh, *all right*! I'm *sorry*. OK?'

The third message was longer. 'Look. Listen. I'm going to the café *now*. It's twenty to six. I'll wait there till seven. If you don't come, OK, I'll just know that's *it*. Right?' And the phone was slammed down.

It was just before six o'clock now. It wouldn't take more than forty minutes once I got to the station; there were plenty of trains at rush hour. I yelled at Dad in the kitchen and he yelled back. I was not to be later than nine o'clock, it was a school day tomorrow, I knew the rules! And *wrap up* – the barometer was dropping like a stone.

He was right about that. It was freezing outside, ice underfoot and vicious needles of sleet slashing horizontally into my face. I kept my head down, slipping and slithering, but I managed to stay upright. Then I was in the warmth of the Underground station and crashing down the escalators to the Northern Line.

There was a train waiting. I got in, but only just: lucky I'm thin, I thought. Even so, there wasn't much room to breathe. Someone said, 'Cattle, that's all we are, load of meat for the knackers,' and several people laughed, though it didn't seem all that funny. And though I was thin, I wasn't tall enough for this squash: my nose was level with a man's stinky armpit.

Not for long, though. There were only two stops between the Angel station and Bank, which was where I had to change for the Central Line to Notting Hill Gate. Bank was a huge underground station, miles of dim, leaking tunnels and crumbling spiral stairs. (Although there were a few ancient and grubby notices saying a programme of repairs was under way, there were not many people who believed this any longer.)

I knew Bank station. I could have found my way blindfold; up and down, in and out, from the Northern to the Central Line and back again. But this evening the tunnels and stairs were more crowded – and much smellier – than usual. When I started to climb the last flight of dark, winding stairs, there were so many people thundering down them that I had to cling on to the rail at the side with both hands to avoid being knocked over and trampled to death underfoot.

I heard the voice over the Tannoy: '. . . a serious fire at Stratford. There will be no more trains on the Central Line tonight.'

I managed to look at my watch. It was twenty minutes past six. If the trains were not running, there was no other way I could get to the café at Notting Hill by seven o'clock.

I thought, *it's not true*! I went on, hauling myself up the stairs, hand over hand on the rail, fighting against the flood of people, the raging tide.

A man said, as he passed, 'Central Line's closed, don't waste your time.'

I still couldn't believe it. I said, under my breath, 'No, oh, please, no . . .'

I felt a hand under my arm. Someone said, 'Do you want a train? Where do you want to go?'

'Notting Hill Gate. But the Central Line's closed.'

I looked up. Very tall, a very black suit, a very black face, a white shirt, white as a swan's wing. White, white teeth – he was smiling.

I said, 'I have to get there. My granny is dying.'

I don't know why I said that. Perhaps I thought it sounded more important than a quarrel with Tom. Or I was ashamed of the quarrel.

He said, his white smile growing broader, 'Then we'll have to get you there. Find a train.'

I said, 'There aren't any trains. There's been a fire.'

But his hand was firm under my elbow. He was taking the brunt of the downward rush of the crowd on his shoulder, shielding me with his body. Then we were through a tiled arch to the Central Line.

And an empty platform. Just me, and my

rescuer, and the voice from the Tannoy. It said, echoing through the tunnels, 'There will be no more trains on the Central Line tonight.'

My rescuer said, 'It will be all right. Trust me. There will be a train very soon.'

I thought he must be mad. But he looked perfectly sane.

He said, again, 'Trust me.' And, in that very same moment, I heard the distant rattle-bang-roar of the approaching train. Then its lights flashing yellow in the dark of the tunnel, then the swish and the rumble as it drew into the station. And stopped.

The doors opened. Although I could see people on board, no one moved. When we got on, I saw why. There were several men and women in our carriage, and they were all asleep. I sat down on an empty seat and my companion sat opposite. He smiled at me and, as the train started up again, said – speaking softly, as if he didn't want to wake the other passengers, 'It is Notting Hill Gate you want, isn't it?'

I said, 'Yes,' and he nodded, as if setting this down in his memory. Then he closed his eyes and seemed to fall, like everyone else, into a deep, peaceful slumber.

The train didn't stop at St Paul's, or Chancery Lane, or Holborn, or Tottenham Court Road. It slowed down as we went through Oxford Circus, but there was no one waiting on the platform and, in the end, it didn't stop there either. The same thing – no one waiting, the train slowing but not stopping – happened at Bond Street and Marble Arch. But my friend woke up. He said, 'Notting Hill Gate?'

I said, 'Not yet. There's Lancaster Gate and Queensway first.'

I was suddenly beginning to be afraid. There must be something wrong. Perhaps this wasn't a real train but a ghost train, and all the sleeping people were dead. Perhaps they had died in the fire. Perhaps I was dead too.

But I didn't believe in ghosts.

My friend smiled his white smile. He said, 'Please do not worry.'

The train stopped at Queensway. There were two men in the uniform of London Underground on the platform. They turned as the train drew in and I thought they looked puzzled.

I said, hearing my voice rising, high and nervous, 'It's the next stop.'

'I know,' he said. His eyelids drooped and he seemed to doze. But when we arrived at Notting Hill Gate, they snapped open and his dark eyes were bright. 'You will be all right now,' he said.

The doors opened. Two of the passengers, an old man with a black and grey beard, and a boy with a gold stud in his eyebrow, woke up, yawning, looking about them, and then made a rush for the door. They stumbled on to the platform at the same time as I did but they took no notice of me, nor of each other.

The train doors closed with a hiss. And I ran.

I ran up the escalator, up the stairs. There was no one in the ticket hall. The tobacconist and stationer's was boarded up. A sign on a tripod said, 'Station Closed'.

I ran up the dirty concrete steps to the street. There was light and traffic and people. I breathed in exhaust fumes and tasted the lovely smell of real life.

It was five minutes to seven. I hopped from

one foot to another until the red man turned green and went walking; then I flew over the road, a few hundred yards to the café where Tom was waiting.

I didn't tell him. I felt too embarrassed. (And I didn't want him to know that I had minded so much!)

I didn't tell my mother and father either. Not even when they said on the nine o'clock news (I was in at one minute to nine) that the Central Line had been closed from five-thirty this evening and there would be no more trains tonight. All I said was that I knew all about *that*! I had come home on the Circle Line to King's Cross and it had taken me ages.

But I told my grandmother. She listened and smiled and her eyes went misty. She said, 'That was an angel, of course. Either your guardian angel, or the Underground angel. It's good to know they still do a bit of work for their living.'

I said, 'You don't believe that!'

'Can you think of a better explanation?'

I said, ashamed, 'I told him that you were dying.'

She laughed. 'I'm glad you think my death might be important enough to persuade an angel to get on the job so efficiently!'

I said indignantly, 'But it was a lie!'

And she laughed again. She said, 'Any angel worth his salt would know that.'